Cross-e

"So you still refuse to tell me where you got this," Mr. Sheldrake, the assistant principal, said, looking up from the exam booklet on his desk.

"It's like I said, sir," Tony insisted. "I found it in my backpack. I don't know how it got there."

"And you expect me to believe that?" Sheldrake retorted.

"Mr. Sheldrake," Joe said, "Tony and I didn't—"

Sheldrake cut him off. "Until we have decided how to handle this situation, you both are suspended. Is that clear?"

"But, sir—" Tony started to speak.

Sheldrake raised his voice. "This is stolen property, and it was found in your possession. Just be glad I'm not reporting the incident to the police!"

The Hardy Boys Mystery Stories

**Available from MINSTREL Books
and ALADDIN Paperbacks**

THE HARDY BOYS®

#171
THE TEST CASE

FRANKLIN W. DIXON

Aladdin Paperbacks
New York London Toronto Sydney Singapore

This book is a work of fiction. Any references to historical events, real people, or real locales are used fictitiously. Other names, characters, places, and incidents are the product of the author's imagination, and any resemblance to actual events or locales or persons, living or dead, is entirely coincidental.

First Aladdin Paperbacks edition January 2002

Copyright © 2002 by Simon & Schuster, Inc.

ALADDIN PAPERBACKS
An imprint of Simon & Schuster
Children's Publishing Division
1230 Avenue of the Americas
New York, NY 10020

The text of this book was set in New Caledonia.

Printed in the United States of America
2 4 6 8 10 9 7 5 3 1

THE HARDY BOYS and THE HARDY BOYS MYSTERY STORIES are trademarks of Simon & Schuster, Inc.

Library of Congress Control Number: 2001096914

ISBN 0-7434-3738-1

Contents

1 An Icy Spill

Joe Hardy finished tightening the laces on his left ice skate and glanced up. It was a perfect day for a skating party. The sunlight reflecting off the ice was so bright that he had to squint. Across the pond, each naked tree branch stood out black against the cloudless sky.

"Come on, move it!" Joe's older brother, Frank, called. He glided past with his girlfriend, Callie Shaw. Joe noticed Frank was wearing the blue- and red-striped scarf Callie had knit for him. The ends fluttered behind him in the chilly breeze.

"Don't sweat it," Joe called back. "I'll catch up. And pass you guys too!"

When Callie had phoned the Hardys earlier about getting together at the pond in Bayport's

Memorial Park, the brothers jumped at the idea. So had their other friends whom Callie called.

When they got to the park, they found out they weren't the only ones to think of a skating party. The ice was already crowded. Even before he got his skates on, Joe waved to a dozen or more kids he knew from Bayport High School, where he was a junior and Frank a senior.

Humming to himself, Joe bent down to tie the laces on his right skate. Just as he finished, somebody snatched the fleece hat off his head.

"Hey!" Joe exclaimed, and jumped to his feet.

Iola Morton stood a few feet away, a twinkle in her eyes and a smile on her lips. Joe's hat dangled from her outstretched hand. Joe made a grab for it, but Iola skated backward, just far enough to be out of reach.

"Grrr! Just wait!" Joe growled, pretending to be angry.

Iola laughed. She spun around and sped across the ice. Joe took off after her. He was starting to catch up when a skater in a brightly colored parka crossed directly in front of him, missing him by inches.

Joe reacted instantly. He bent his knees and jumped a quarter turn to the left. The blades of his skates caught and scraped sideways across the ice, throwing up a spray of glittering ice chips.

Joe came to a stop and straightened up. He

turned to yell at whoever had almost slammed into him. Too late. The guy was already lost in the crowd.

"Close call," Tony Prito said. He clapped Joe on the shoulder.

Tony was one of Frank and Joe's friends. Wiry and agile, he played second base on the Bayport High School baseball team.

"Too bad you didn't accidentally stick out your foot and trip him," Tony added, shaking his head. "Though he's pretty used to that kind of thing."

"Why? Do you know him?" Joe asked. "Who is he?"

"Don't ask me. You're the detective," Tony replied with a grin.

Joe grinned back. He didn't mind being teased. He and his brother, Frank, had a growing reputation for solving mysteries, which they came by naturally. Their dad was Fenton Hardy, a famous private detective. When they were younger, he had sometimes asked them for help on tough cases. Soon Frank and Joe were investigating crimes on their own.

"I'm off duty today," Joe said. "Come on, give. Who is that dude?"

"Okay, okay. His name's Carl Shute," Tony replied. "We had history together last year, but we didn't exactly hit it off. He's a starter on the hockey team."

"Oh?" Joe said. "Any good?"

Tony hesitated. "Well . . . if you ask me, his playing stinks. But he's got a way with his elbows and stick."

"I hear you," Joe said, and wrinkled his nose. He liked watching hockey, but if a brawl broke out, it turned him off. When he wanted to see a fight, he went to a martial arts tournament.

Iola skated over to join them. She slid Joe's hat back on his head, then tucked an arm through his. "Well?" she said. "Are we skating or what?"

Joe grinned down at her. "What," he replied. He took her by the waist and lifted her off her feet.

"That's enough of the he-man stuff," Iola said. She grabbed the edge of his fleece hat and pulled it down over his eyes. "How do you like it in the dark, big guy?"

"I give up!" Joe said. He set her down gently, then pushed up his hat. "Let's do some skating."

Just then Frank and Callie skated up with two other friends, Biff Hooper and Chet Morton. Chet was Iola's older brother. Joe, Iola, and Tony joined them in circling the pond a couple of times. Then they stopped to watch some kids who were ice dancing to the sound of a boom box.

"Out of my way!" someone yelled. Two guys pushed through the spectators and raced across the dance area. They barely missed one of the dancers. Angry shouts followed them as they took off.

Joe looked over and caught Tony's eye. "Same guy, right?" he called.

"Right," Tony answered. "The other dude's named Brad Austin. He's on the hockey team too."

"What a couple of turkeys!" Frank said in disgust. "Do they think they own the pond?"

"No, just the ice," Callie said. "Forget them. Let's do something fun. How about crack-the-whip?"

A few other people joined them. Joe took a turn at anchor and another at the far end of the whip. He was amazed at how fast he went when the whip cracked. He crouched down and cannoned across the ice, carefully avoiding other skaters. He came to a stop a few yards from the two hockey players.

"Hey, hot dog," the one named Carl said with a scowl. "Why don't you watch where you're going?"

Joe didn't want to spoil the afternoon with a fight. Instead, he gave Carl a steady look and said, "Good advice. For everyone." He turned and skated back to his friends.

"Hey, everybody, look!" Iola called. She pulled a Frisbee out of Chet's backpack. "Anybody remember how to play Monkey in the Middle?"

Joe soon realized that catching a Frisbee on skates was tricky. Everyone took at least one spill. When it was Chet's turn in the middle of the ring, Callie made a toss that seemed to hover a foot above his head. Chet raised both arms and jumped for the Frisbee. He caught it, but when he came down, his skates slithered in different directions, sending him flat on the ice.

Everyone rushed to help him. "Chet!" Callie exclaimed. "Are you okay?"

Chet sat up. "Of course I am," he said in a dignified voice. "Don't you realize how privileged you are? You've just seen the world's first successful triple klutz!"

All of them cracked up except Biff, who looked puzzled. Iola explained that there was a skating jump called a triple lutz. Biff let out a loud guffaw just as the others stopped laughing.

Next it was Tony's turn in the middle. Frank tossed the Frisbee across the ring to Callie. A gust of wind carried it past her, and she had to skate after it. Just as she bent down to pick it up, Carl zoomed past and nudged her. Callie recoiled and lost her balance.

While Frank skated over to help her up, Joe raced after the careless hockey player. "Hey, man!" he shouted. "How about you watch where you're going!"

Carl spun around, fists clenched. "You talking to me?" he demanded.

"You better believe I am," Joe replied. He stopped an arm's length from Carl. "You just knocked down my friend. Don't you think you ought to tell her you're sorry?"

6

Carl eyed Joe's six-foot muscular build. He didn't seem pleased by what he saw. "I didn't notice her," he mumbled. "Anyway, I barely bumped her."

Carl's friend, Brad, skated over. "Hey, we don't want any trouble," he said. "Right, Carl? A fun afternoon is all."

"Yeah, right," Carl muttered. "Tell the chick I'm sorry."

Joe thought of a few good replies to this. Before he could get any of them out, Carl spun around and skated off. Brad gave Joe a shrug, then followed his bud.

"Hey, why don't you all come over to my house for cocoa and cookies?" Callie said a little later.

"All right!" Chet exclaimed. "Nothing like exercise to work up an appetite."

"Not that you need much help with that," Iola said jokingly. The others laughed. Chet had never met a snack he didn't like.

At Callie's they sat in a semicircle in front of the living room fireplace. Callie tossed a pinecone on the fire, which turned the flames blue, green, and yellow.

Joe told about his conversation with Carl. "Can you believe that guy?" he said at the end. "What a jerk!"

"Forget him," Chet told him. "We've got bigger things to worry about. Personally I'm worried about the SAB."

The SAB was the State Achievement Battery, a standardized test of language and math. According to a new state law, all high school students had to take it. Their scores would appear on their permanent school records.

"Did you have to mention that?" Iola complained. "On a weekend?"

"Chet's right," Tony said. "That test's something to worry about. If you don't do well, it could spoil your chances of going to a good college."

"It could be bad for the school, too," Callie said. "Unless enough kids score at grade level or above, we could lose all kinds of state aid. We could even be knocked out of statewide sports competitions."

"They wouldn't do that, would they?" Biff asked. "That would be so unfair. Bayport's got state-ranked teams in half a dozen different sports."

"Hey, don't sweat it," Frank said. "We rank pretty high academically. Just look at the colleges last year's seniors got into."

"I'm not worried about how Bayport High will do," Tony said. "I'm worried about how Tony Prito will do. I fall apart on these fill-in-the-bubble tests."

Callie gave him a sympathetic look. "I know about that," she said. "Tests are one big pain. But we've still got next week to practice."

"I heard of a way to raise your score a lot," Iola said. "But it costs big bucks."

"You mean, prep courses?" Biff asked. "Sure. But you have to put in months on them. A few days every week after school and weekends, too. That'd be great if we'd thought of it in time. But now we've only got a few days left."

Iola shook her head. "I'm not talking about prep courses. The other day I overheard two girls talking in the third-floor girl's room. They didn't know I was there. One of them said she knew where to buy a copy of the test. Five hundred dollars, she said."

Biff whistled in amazement. Chet said, "How about five dollars? If I smash my piggy bank, I think I could swing that much."

"Where? How?" Frank asked, his detective instincts aroused. "That's illegal. Would you know the girls again?"

"No, sorry," Iola told him. "Someone else came in then, and the girls shut up and left. I didn't even get a look at them."

On Monday Joe's fourth-period American history class was supposed to watch a videotape about westward expansion. But when Ms. Holder started the tape, the title that appeared on the monitor was *How We See: The Amazing Story of Vision.*

Ms. Holder stopped the tape, ejected it, and turned to Joe. "Um, Joe?" she said. "Would you mind taking this down to the media center and bringing back the correct cassette?"

"Sure," Joe said, glad to get up and move.

The media center was on the ground floor, in the same wing as the athletic complex. Joe exchanged the tape for the right one and started back. The hallway was empty, and as he passed the gym, Tony came out.

"Hey," Joe said, "what's up?"

"Had to see Coach, and then he let me shoot some hoops," Tony replied as he joined Joe walking down the hall. "Hey, remember I was telling you about this cool new Italian motorcycle? I found a magazine article about it. Great photos. Want to see?"

"You bet," Joe told him. "But just a glance. I have to get back to class."

Tony stopped and opened his backpack and rummaged inside. "Hey, what's this?" he asked. He pulled out a printed booklet sealed in shrink-wrapped plastic. A small piece of paper was stuck to the front by static electricity. Tony brushed the paper back into his bag and added, "Where'd this come from?"

Joe looked. The cover of the booklet read *State Achievement Battery—Part I*.

"Uh-oh," Joe said. "I don't think you're supposed to have that."

"I don't either," Tony replied. "But how—"

"May I see your passes?" a voice asked. "Why aren't you two in class?"

A teacher stood staring at them suspiciously. Joe had seen her around but did not know her name. He was about to explain about exchanging the cassettes for Ms. Holder when the teacher's eye fell on the booklet in Tony's hand. She caught her breath.

"What's that?" she demanded. She grabbed it and looked it over front and back.

"You'd better come with me to the principal's office," she added grimly. "You boys are in big trouble!"

2 Suspended Education

"Do you have any idea what a serious matter this is?" Mr. Sheldrake asked, looking up from the exam booklet on his desk. "If you don't, you're going to find out very fast."

Mr. Sheldrake was the assistant principal, and he had been given the nickname Old Beady Eyes.

"So you still refuse to tell me where you got this," Sheldrake continued.

"It's like I said, sir," Tony replied. "I found it in my backpack. I don't know how it got there."

"And you expect me to believe that?" Sheldrake retorted. "I'm sorry, I wasn't born yesterday. The moment Mr. Chambers gets back from his meeting, I'm going to tell him this whole story. I assure you, he won't take it lightly."

Mr. Chambers was the principal. The word around school was that he kept his nice guy rep by letting Sheldrake handle all the dirty work.

"Mr. Sheldrake," Joe said, "Tony and I didn't—"

Sheldrake cut him off. "Until we have decided how to handle this, you both are suspended. You will leave the school property at once, and you will not communicate with any other students at Bayport High School. Is that clear?"

"But, sir—" Tony started to speak.

Sheldrake raised his voice. "This is stolen property, and it was found in your possession. Just be glad I'm not reporting the incident to the police!"

"Sir," Joe said, "you don't mean I can't talk to my brother, do you?"

The school official hesitated, then said, "No, that wouldn't be reasonable. But remember, under no circumstances are you to say a single word to him about the contents of this exam. Not one word! Is that clear?"

"I didn't even look at the booklet," Joe said. "And neither did Tony. You can see for yourself. It's in a sealed package."

"These things can be opened and resealed," Sheldrake said ominously. "That's it. We'll be in touch with you and your parents. One of the security people will see you off the premises."

"What about our schoolwork?" Tony asked. "We don't want to fall behind."

"You will come to this office every day after school to turn in your assignments and receive the next day's work," Sheldrake said.

The assistant principal picked up the phone and murmured something into it. A few moments later one of the school guards tapped on the door and came in. "Ah, Mr. Robinson," Sheldrake said. "You will escort these two young men off the premises. Be sure they don't speak to any other students."

"Yes, sir," Robinson said. "Okay, boys, follow me."

Joe remembered the videotape in his hand. "Will you see that Ms. Holder gets this?" he asked, placing the cassette on Sheldrake's desk. Sheldrake glared and did not reply.

The bell rang as they left the office, and the hallways filled up at once. Joe saw people turn to watch as he and Tony went by with their guard. A guy from the baseball team called out, "Hey, Tony, what's up?"

Tony shook his head but didn't answer.

Joe kept glancing around, hoping to spot Frank. Just as he was about to give up, he saw him coming down the stairs. Frank noticed Joe and pushed through the crowd to his side.

"Joe!" he exclaimed. "What's the matter?"

"No talking," the guard said, looking uncomfortable. "Stand back, please."

"Call me at home," Joe yelled over his shoulder as the guard hustled them away.

14

Outside, Joe and Tony paused before going in different directions.

"My parents are going to kill me," Tony moaned. "Or kill themselves. Maybe both!"

"We didn't do anything wrong," Joe said.

"So what?" Tony retorted. "We got suspended, didn't we? That's what counts."

"Not if we can prove we're innocent," Joe said. "And the best way to do that is to find out how that test booklet got in your backpack. Somebody put it there, and once we figure out who, the case is solved."

Tony's face brightened. "Hey, that's right! I've been trying to figure this out. I know it wasn't there third period. I went through everything trying to find a note I'd misplaced. So that means it must have been put there while I was in the gym."

"What did you do with your backpack while you were on the court?" Joe asked.

"Left it on the floor near the sidelines," Tony replied.

"You didn't see anybody messing with it, did you?"

"Hey, I was shooting baskets," Tony told him.

The guard hurried down the walk toward them. "Sorry, fellows," he said. "My orders are to send you home. No loitering around the school. Don't give me a hard time, okay?"

Joe raised his hands and said, "Okay, okay. We're going."

As they walked off, Joe turned to Tony. In an undertone he said, "Call me when you get home. We need to make some plans."

Joe was not used to walking home from school, but he told himself the exercise was good for him. At home, he found his aunt Gertrude, making lunch. Her jaw dropped to see him in the middle of the day.

"What's this?" she demanded. "Are you sick? Do you want me to call the doctor?"

"I'm okay, Aunt Gertrude," Joe said quickly. "A little problem with the school officials, that's all. Is Mom or Dad around?"

"Your mother went into the city to have lunch with a friend," Aunt Gertrude told him. "She'll be back before dinnertime, I expect. And your father was called down to Washington for a couple of days on business. When I was growing up, people didn't zip around the country this way. It makes me dizzy."

Joe felt a tiny sense of relief. With a lot of luck and hard work, he might solve his problem before he had to tell his parents.

The phone rang. "I'll get it," Joe said, picking up the receiver. "Hello?"

"What's going on?" Frank demanded. "People are saying you and Tony were expelled for cheating!"

"Not exactly," Joe replied. He explained what had happened, then said, "Since I'm not allowed to

16

talk to anyone at school; you'll have to handle that part of the investigation."

"I'll get right on it," Frank said. "We can work out what to do next when I get home. And, hey, don't sweat it. We'll ace this problem in no time."

Frank intercepted Callie and Iola on their way into the cafeteria. He told them about the trouble Joe and Tony were in, then said, "We need to find out all about those tests. Where are they kept? If here at school, when did they get here? How could somebody get hold of one and put it in Tony's pack?"

"And why?" Callie added. "That's an even bigger mystery, if you ask me."

"Doris, the secretary in the student affairs office, is one of my mom's friends," Iola said. "You guys go to lunch. I'll see what she can tell me and meet you inside."

"We'll get you a sandwich," Callie told her.

Chet Morton and Phil Cohen were already at their usual table. Frank filled them in.

"Old Beady Eyes must be sweating," Chet observed. "The last thing Bayport High needs is a cheating scandal. I bet he tries to hush it up."

"Sure," Callie said. "That must be why he won't let Joe and Tony talk to anyone."

"No," Phil said. "I think it's 'cause he's scared they'll give us the answers."

"You know what Iola told us yesterday," Frank said. "Have any of you heard about copies of the test floating around? Or about ways to get a better score on it?"

The others shook their heads.

"Well, ask around, okay?" Frank continued. "I don't know why Tony and Joe got dragged into this, but that test is all we've got."

Iola came into the lunchroom then and joined them. "All right," she said in a low voice. "The boxes of tests were delivered to the school last Thursday. They were locked in a storeroom, and they've been there ever since. *But*"—she leaned forward—"word is, one of the boxes was opened!"

"Great work, Iola!" Frank exclaimed. He glanced up at the clock on the wall. "Callie, let's go talk to whoever's in charge of the loading dock. Maybe the box was open when the tests came."

The receiving area was down the hall from the cafeteria kitchen. Frank and Callie edged around dollies stacked with supplies and walked down a ramp to the loading platform. The big overhead door to the outside was down, but a chilly breeze blew in through a smaller side door, which was wedged open.

A balding man in khakis was working at a cluttered table inside a windowed booth next to the doors. A small electric heater glowed near him. Frank noticed the name Mel embroidered above the pocket of the man's shirt as he tapped on the glass.

Mel stood up and opened the door of the booth. "Yeah?" he said. "What do you need?"

Frank introduced himself and Callie, then said, "We're doing a paper on the way sensitive materials are handled at Bayport High. Somebody said we should ask you about the state tests that came last week."

Mel's face closed up. "I don't have anything to say about that."

"But there *are* special procedures for things like that, aren't there?" Callie asked.

"We got rules here," Mel said. He waved toward the table. "Rules for every kind of situation—and we follow them."

"Can you give us an example?" Frank asked. "Say a truck pulls up with cartons of tests. Then what happens?"

"What happens? Well, the driver off-loads the shipment. I check it against the bill of lading. Here, like this." Mel reached over and picked up a flimsy sheet of yellow paper from the top of a stack of similar sheets.

Frank quickly looked it over. The shipper was the State Education Authority, the contents were six cartons described as "Achievement Battery," and the date was the previous week. He memorized the number printed in red in the upper corner.

"So if it's all there, I sign for it." Mel concluded. "If it isn't, I don't. Now, if you kids don't mind, I've got work to do."

Callie gave him a big smile. "Thanks for your help," she said.

Mel turned back to the table. Frank noticed him pick up a walkie-talkie and thumb the talk button. He grabbed Callie's arm and pulled her out of sight, then put a finger to his lips.

"Come in, Ramon," Mel said in a voice that carried. "That shipment of tests that showed up last Thursday. . . . Yeah. . . . Don't let on they sat unguarded in the loading bay for almost an hour. You hear? That's strictly between you and me. If it was to get out, it could cost us our jobs!"

Joe's detective experience had taught him that people often forgot important details of events. He sat and tried to jot down everything he remembered from the moment he had run into Tony near the gym until the guard had hustled them out of the building. He was frowning and gnawing the end of his pencil when the phone rang.

Aunt Gertrude answered it. A moment later she called, "Joe? For you. A young lady."

Joe went to the phone. "Hello?"

"Hi, Joe, it's Liz Webling."

Joe made a face. He knew Liz from school. She wrote for the *Beacon,* the school paper, and now

20

and then got to appear on a local cable news show. Her father ran the *Bayport Times,* and Liz saw herself as a hotshot, dig-up-the-dirt reporter. Other people saw her as a pain.

"Liz, I can't talk to you," Joe said.

"I'll call back," Liz replied. "I want your comment on the rumors that you are part of a cheating ring."

"I can't talk to you," Joe repeated.

Liz pretended not to hear. "Is it true that you've been suspended from school?" she asked. "How do you feel about that? Are you concerned that this might eventually keep you from being admitted to the college of your choice?"

Gently Joe placed the receiver on the cradle. He wiggled his lower jaw to loosen it, then cracked his knuckles. He felt like hitting a wall.

The phone rang again. "Aunt Gertrude?" Joe called. "Don't get that. Let the machine answer."

From the answering machine in his father's study, Joe heard Liz say, in a goody-goody voice, "If I were you, Joe Hardy, I'd be sure to watch the Bayport Cable News tonight. Seven o'clock on Channel Sixty-one. If you miss it, you'll be sorry!"

When seven o'clock came around, Joe, Frank, their mom, and Aunt Gertrude gathered near the TV. Joe put a fresh cassette in the VCR and started recording.

The top story was about a local zoning dispute. Next was an interview with a former mayor of Bayport who had turned eighty. Then Liz came on. She explained briefly what the State Achievement Battery was and why the scores were important. Then came clips of her talking to a Bayport High student. The student's face was in shadow, and his voice was electronically distorted. He told her he had been offered a copy of the test for five hundred dollars.

"It sounds like Iola was on to something," Joe remarked.

"Shhh!" Frank hissed.

"School officials refused to speak to us, and our cameras were barred from Bayport High School," Liz continued dramatically. "However, here is a Bayport Cable News exclusive. We have learned that two Bayport students are being investigated for possible involvement in an organized cheating ring."

She paused and smirked at the camera. "We also have this solid lead from an informed source. One of the students alleged to be involved is known far beyond Bayport High School. Why? Because of his highly publicized activities as an amateur detective!"

3 Scores for Sale

Frank used the remote to turn off the TV.

Joe pounded his fist into his palm. "Can you believe that!" he exclaimed. "While she was at it, why didn't she give my address and phone number too!"

He grabbed the telephone.

"What are you doing?" Frank asked.

"Calling Liz Webling," Joe replied. "I'm going to tell her exactly how low I think she is."

Frank took a deep breath. "Hold on, Joe," he said. "I don't think that's a good idea. First of all, Sheldrake ordered you not to talk to other students. Second, you can bet Liz will tape every word you say and play it on tomorrow night's show."

"Do you expect me to sit here and do nothing?" Joe protested.

"What do you think?" Frank asked, giving his younger brother a steady look.

Joe let out a loud breath. "All right," he said. "The best way for us to deal with a turkey like Liz is to get to the truth first. Is that what you expect me to say?"

Frank grinned. "Is that what you think?"

Joe aimed a friendly punch at Frank's shoulder. Frank swayed backward and let it swoosh past.

Aunt Gertrude looked worried. "I don't understand," she said. "Boys, was that girl on the TV talking about you? There was something almost nasty in her manner."

"It's okay," Joe told her. "Just a misunderstanding. Don't let it bother you."

"Well, it bothers *me*," Laura Hardy said. "I intend to call Mr. Chambers first thing tomorrow morning. I don't understand why he didn't get in touch with us right away. It's no small thing to suspend a student from high school. Even if you manage to keep up with your classes, it leaves a black mark on your record. That's not right."

"I know," Joe said. "I don't like it one bit, believe me. But if we can show Chambers and Sheldrake what really happened, they'll have to back down. The worst part is, practically all the suspects and witnesses are at school, and I'm not allowed to talk to anyone. It's like trying to juggle with both hands tied."

"We'll split up the investigation," Frank said. "You and Tony handle everything outside school. The rest of the gang and I will take on the inside work."

A few minutes later the phone rang. Frank picked it up. "Hello?"

"Frank, it's Callie. I'm so mad at Liz!" she declared. "Talk about conniving and underhanded! And do you know, she left a message on my voice mail telling me to watch? I wonder how many other people she called. Lots, I bet."

"It wouldn't surprise me," Frank replied.

"I've been phoning around since I got home." Callie continued. "So far I've found three kids who got calls offering to sell them a copy of the SAB."

"Way to go!" Frank exclaimed. "What did they tell you?"

"The calls all came on Friday or over the weekend," Callie told him. "The price was always five hundred dollars. And two people told me the guy who called had a gruff voice."

"As if he was disguising it?" Frank asked.

"Yeah, probably," Callie said. "But here's the best part. This girl, Michelle, she got her call on Saturday morning. After she turned the guy down, she got curious. She punched the code to redial the last caller. Guess who answered?"

"Elvis Presley?" Frank said.

Callie laughed. "The Bayport High switchboard. The call came from inside school."

"So whoever called was at school on Saturday morning, with access to a phone," Frank said excitedly. "Did you find out what time?"

"Yes, around eleven o'clock," Callie replied.

"That's a big clue!" Frank said. "Thanks, Callie. Good work."

Just minutes after Frank finished talking to Callie, the phone rang again. This time it was Chet.

"I've been calling people, the way we agreed," Chet said. "And I've got some news."

"Offers to sell a copy of the test?" Frank asked.

"What? No," Chet replied. "But a bunch of kids have been getting calls from a tutoring service. An outfit called U-Score-Hi. The guy's name is Sal Martin. He said he could raise their scores on the SAB with just one prep session. Sounds fishy to me."

"Me too," Frank said. "Did any of them say anything about his voice?"

"How did you know?" Chet asked. "A couple of people told me he sounded like a pretty tough customer. According to Mark Kaminsky, he talked like somebody on a gangster show. Not what you'd expect from a tutor. Also, he was asking for two hundred bucks for one session. That's crazy."

"Did anybody sign up with him?" Frank asked.

"If they did, they weren't admitting it. I'll try some more people and let you know what I find out tomorrow," Chet answered.

Frank told Joe what Callie and Chet had learned.

Joe reached for the Bayport telephone book.

"Here it is," he announced. "U-Score-Hi. It's over on Markham Street. Let's see if they're in the yellow pages."

"Are they?" Frank inquired.

Joe laughed. "Believe it! They say they prepare people for high school equivalency exams, civil service tests, and the written test for commercial drivers' licenses. Pretty broadband outfit."

"Hold on," Frank said. "Think back a couple of months. Wasn't Dad talking about crooks who were selling the answers to driving tests?"

"Hey, that's right," Joe said. "They had the answers printed on watchbands or something. You think this is the same gang?"

"Sounds like it," Frank said. "If so, it seems they're trying to break into the high school market."

"But how do you sell the answers if you don't have them? This is the first time the SAB has been given."

"You get hold of the test and figure out the answers," Frank replied. "And I'd guess that's exactly what somebody's doing."

The next morning over breakfast Joe and Frank went over their plans and arranged times to talk by phone. Joe dropped Frank off at school, then drove back to the house. It felt strange to be home on a schoolday and not be sick. He dialed Tony's number.

"Hey, Joe," Tony said, "any news?"

"Not a lot," Joe replied. "How about you?"

"I am totally grounded," Tony announced. "My parents just about had a cow when they heard I was suspended."

"Didn't you tell them you didn't do it?" Joe asked, shocked.

"Sure I did," Tony said. "My dad said it didn't matter: If you try to fight city hall, you lose, no matter who's right. They told me I have to stay home and study full-time."

"Get out! That's really tough," Joe said. "What about your job?"

Tony worked after school at Mr. Pizza, a favorite hangout for Bayport students.

"I told them I'd lose my job if I didn't show up," Tony replied. "So they said okay, I can go in to work. But afterward I come straight home. I'm sorry, Joe, but I can't help with the investigation. I just hope you and Frank find out who put that stupid test in my pack."

"We'll do our best," Joe said.

After the phone call to Tony, Joe logged on to the Internet and searched for the Web site of the express company that had delivered the tests to the school. As he hoped, there was a feature that allowed customers to track shipments. He entered the number Frank had copied from the bill of lading and held his breath.

Within seconds the information appeared on the screen. The six cartons had been picked up at the State Education Authority on the previous Monday at 2:38 P.M. After several transfers they had reached the Bayport distribution center early Thursday morning. They had been put on a truck that left just after noon and had been signed for at the school at 4:22 P.M.

Joe copied the information into his notebook, then searched the site for the telephone number of the Bayport office and dialed it.

"Hi, could I speak to the dispatcher, please?" he asked.

"Please hold," the operator said. Some tinkly music came on.

After half a minute or so there was a loud click. "Kelly here," a voice said.

"Hi, Mr. Kelly," Joe said. "This is Joe Hardy, from Bayport High School. We took a delivery from you last Thursday afternoon. Can you tell me the name of the driver who delivered them?"

"Is there a problem?" Kelly asked.

"No, no," Joe said quickly. "After he left, we found a pair of sunglasses. We thought he might have dropped them."

"Oh. Let's see. . . ." After a pause Kelly said, "That would be Fred Adolphus. But I doubt if they're his. He doesn't usually wear sunglasses. He should be back around eleven. I'll ask him."

"Thanks," Joe said, and hung up. He smelled something baking in the kitchen and got there just as his aunt Gertrude was taking a batch of peanut butter cookies from the oven. He poured a glass of milk, then snitched a hot cookie. He jiggled it in his hand to keep from burning his fingers.

"Oh, you!" Aunt Gertrude protested. "No patience at all!"

Joe grinned. "Why be patient around cookies this good?" He grabbed another and retreated before his aunt could react.

The phone rang. It was Frank. Joe told him what he had learned from the express company.

"Great," Frank said. "You going to try to catch the driver and question him?"

"Does a bear sleep in the woods?" Joe replied with a laugh.

"Everybody's upset about your suspension," Frank said. "People asked me to tell you so. Some guy who knows you from English class wants to hold a demonstration, with signs and all."

"Cool!" Joe exclaimed. "I can hear it now: 'Hey-hey, ho-ho, free Tony, free Joe!' What did you say?"

"I hope I talked him out of it," Frank said. "The last thing we want is to back Old Beady Eyes into a corner. He might not even listen to whatever we find out."

"*Have* you found out anything?" Joe asked.

"Maybe," Frank replied. "I think— Oops, gotta run. I'm late for class. I'll call you later."

"Okay," Joe said. He hung up, put on his coat, and went out to the van. On the way through the kitchen he snared another cookie.

The express company distribution center was in an industrial park on the far side of town. A weed-choked railway siding ran along the back of the building. At the side was a long concrete loading dock with spaces for half a dozen trucks. Three of them were occupied.

Joe parked in a visitors' slot near the front entrance and walked around to the side. A man in blue work clothes was wheeling a pallet of cardboard cartons onto a truck. He eyed Joe curiously.

"Hi," Joe said, with what he hoped was a disarming smile. "Is Fred Adolphus around?"

The man gestured with his thumb at the last parking space. "That van's his," he said. "He should be along in a minute."

Joe walked over to the van. The double doors at the back were open. Inside, cartons were stacked along both side walls. A narrow space between them led up to the driver's seat.

"I hear you're looking for me," a voice said.

Joe turned. The guy facing him was about five-ten, with dark hair and an olive complexion. He looked to be in his early twenties.

On the way over Joe had decided how to approach the driver. He smiled and said, "Hi, Fred.

I'm Joe Hardy, and I'd like your help. I'm a student at Bayport High, and I'm doing a paper for social studies on transportation."

Fred's face relaxed. "Oh, yeah? I went to Bayport. What do you need?"

"The idea is to follow the route a package takes, from beginning to end," Joe explained. He pulled a notebook from his hip pocket and opened it to a blank page.

"I chose some stuff that arrived at the school last week." Joe continued. "So far I've tracked it all the way from the sender to the warehouse here. Now I need to find out about the last step."

"Sure, I made a delivery to the high school last week," Fred said. "Must have been Wednesday or Thursday. My log will tell me."

He went to the front of the van and returned with his logbook. "Let's see. . . . Yeah, here it is." He showed Joe the page. "I left here around noon. The high school was my next to last stop."

Joe looked over the page. "So you delivered a package downtown at two-forty, then reached the high school at three fifty-five? Isn't that a pretty long time for a short trip?"

Fred laughed. "It would have been if I'd gone straight there," he said. "But I took a break on the way for a slice of pizza."

"Sounds good," Joe said. "I'm kind of puzzled, though. The guy at the school showed me a paper that said the packages arrived at four twenty-two, not three fifty-five."

"You're quite a detective, aren't you?" Fred observed. "Yeah, that's right. I got there at three fifty-five, just like my log says, but no one was around. I had to go hunting for them. It took me a quarter hour to find them and turn over the packages. Not the first time that's happened either."

"So while you were looking for them, where was the delivery?" Joe asked.

"On the loading dock, stacked on a hand truck," Fred replied. "Listen, Joe, you need anything else from me? I'm running late."

"No, that's great," Joe said. He closed his notebook. As he started to turn, he thought of something else. "Fred, where did you stop for pizza?"

"Oh, a place we used to go to all the time when I was in high school," Fred said. "You must know it. You probably hang out there yourself. It's called Mr. Pizza."

Joe stared at him. Of course he knew Mr. Pizza. That was where Tony worked.

4   Questions Without Answers

Frank finished his telephone call with Joe and glanced at the big clock on the wall. He had three minutes to get to his next class—just enough time for a quick call to Tony. He dropped some change in the phone and dialed the number.

Tony answered on the first ring. "I know I'm not supposed to talk to you," Frank told him. "But I need to know what your book bag looks like."

"Oh, sure," Tony replied. "It's orange, and the straps are black. On the front is a black mesh pocket with a vertical black stripe. The company's logo is on a blue patch on the flap of the pocket. It makes it easier to pick out. I haven't seen many others like it."

"Great," Frank said. "And as far as you know, the

test must have been put in your bag during fourth period?"

"Right," Tony said. "I'm pretty sure it wasn't there before then. Frank? You think you can get anywhere with this? Having a suspension on my record doesn't look good."

"I'll do my best, you know that," Frank said. "Gotta go," he added as the bell rang.

Frank hung up and dashed down the hall to calculus. Ms. Grusak, the instructor, hated students to come in late. Today, however, *she* was late. Frank settled into his seat and said hi to Chet, who sat next to him.

"I've got a really hot lead," Chet muttered. The door swung open, and Ms. Grusak hurried in. "I'll tell you after class."

Frank had trouble paying attention to math. His mind kept wandering. The sound of his own name brought him back.

"I'm sorry?" he said to Ms. Grusak. "I didn't hear the question."

"I asked you what you noticed about this equation," Ms. Grusak said.

Frank made a wild stab. "Er, it's linear?"

Several students laughed. Obviously that wasn't the right answer. It wasn't even a reasonable wrong answer.

Ms. Grusak gave him a disappointed look and called on someone else. Frank sat up straighter and pushed his thoughts about the investigation into a far corner of his mind. He did not intend to get caught napping a second time.

When class finally ended, Frank turned to Chet. "So what's this hot lead?" he demanded.

"Whoever's trying to sell copies of the test is keeping really busy," Chet replied. "I've got a list of people he's called."

"Same guy?" Frank asked. "Gruff voice, five hundred bucks?"

"Right," Chet said. "One or two calls last night, five or six on Sunday afternoon and evening."

"Maybe because that's when people were home," Frank said.

"Maybe," Chet said. "But here's the big deal. Marcy Canova, a girl I know from Spanish, has caller ID on her phone. She had the sense to write down the number. Here. I've got to run." He handed Frank a scrap of paper and left.

Frank studied the number. It did not look like one of the school numbers. Another lead to check out. Luckily he had a free period coming up, followed by early lunch. He gathered his books and left the room.

"Frank, wait!" Iola called, from down the hall. Frank waited. With Iola was a guy whose bleached blond hair was cut short on top and long in the back. He was wearing baggy jeans and an oversize

T-shirt. A shiny chain led from a belt loop to the wallet in his back pocket.

"I was hoping we'd catch you," Iola said. "This is Brendan. Brendan, tell Frank what you told me."

"Hey, okay," Brendan drawled. "So this dude calls me Sunday night, okay? And he's like, you want to buy a copy of the big test? Only five bills. So I go, hey, man, I'm in."

Frank whistled. "You told him you'd buy it for five hundred dollars? Seriously?"

"Naw, man, I was just goofing with him, you know?" Brendan said hastily. "You don't catch me buying a hot test. That's asking for major grief. Besides, who cares?"

"What happened then?" Frank asked.

"Well, that's what's so weird," Brendan said. He scratched behind his ear. "I figure he's going to tell me how to pass him the loot and all. No way. Instead he just hangs up on me."

Frank stared. "He did? He didn't call back?"

"Unh-unh. Not a peep. You know what I think?" Brendan went on. "There I am goofing with him, and the whole time this jerk is goofing with me!"

Brendan went off to class. Iola stayed a minute longer. "How's Joe doing?" she asked, worried. "He must hate being treated so unfairly."

"He's keeping busy," Frank told her. "That's the best thing he can do, if you ask me."

"Did what Brendan said help any?" Iola asked.

"I think so," Frank replied. "I don't know exactly what it means, but I've got a strong feeling it's something important. Do you want another assignment? Ask around if anyone has a grudge against Tony. Any recent arguments, stuff like that. We'll get together and compare notes at lunch."

"Okay," Iola said. "And when you talk to Joe, tell him to keep his spirits up. We'll beat this thing. Everyone will see what an idiot that Sheldrake is!"

Iola left. Frank went down to the gym and looked over the schedule for the day before. The groups that had been signed up to use it during fourth period, when Tony was there, were girls' JV volleyball and boys' varsity ice hockey.

Only the hockey team had a time slot today as well, for the next period. Girls' volleyball met again on Wednesday during fourth period.

Frank's next stop was the student computer lab. He sat down at a free machine, logged on to the Internet, and surfed until he found a reverse telephone directory that gave the name and address for a specific phone number. In Frank's experience, a lot of the time it didn't work. But when it did, it could be a huge help.

Frank typed in the number Chet had given him and hit enter. After a two-second pause he had his answer. The number belonged to a pay phone, no address given.

With a sigh Frank logged off and went out into the hall. The nearest working pay phone was at the other end of the building. He hiked over and dialed the number. It rang and rang. He was about to give up when someone answered. There were loud traffic noises in the background.

Frank made up a name on the spot. "Hello, is this Coleman's Cleaners?"

"Sorry, wrong number," a man said. "This is a phone booth at the gas station on Franklin and Pershing."

"Sorry," Frank said, and hung up. He jotted down the information in his notebook. The location was in a run-down area of Bayport. Joe could check it out during the afternoon.

A teacher who looked familiar came over to Frank. "What are you doing here?" he asked. "Shouldn't you be in class?"

"I'm a senior," Frank explained, and produced his schedule. Seniors at Bayport High School were allowed to decide how to spend their free periods.

"Well, Frank," the teacher said, after studying the schedule and noting his name, "I know you're within your rights, but I'd rather you didn't hang out in the halls. It gives the younger students the wrong impression. If you're at loose ends, why not go to the library or the student government office?"

"Thanks, I'll do that," Frank said. Instead he went down to the security desk near the front entrance. He was in luck. The guard on duty was a guy he occasionally stopped to talk sports with.

"Hi, Marcus," Frank said. "How's it going?"

"Can't complain," Marcus replied. "What's new with you?"

"I'm hoping you can help me win a bet," Frank said. "Saturday morning I thought I spotted a friend of mine out at the mall with a girl who is *not* his girlfriend. He swears he was here at school, working on a project. Saturdays everybody who enters the building has to sign in, right?"

"That's the rule," the guard told him.

"So if my bud was here, his name's in the log?" Frank continued. "Mind if I look?"

"Help yourself," Marcus said. He thumbed back through the pages of the big book. "Here we are, Saturday morning. Not that many customers."

The front door opened, and a man came in. He was holding an envelope and an unfolded letter. He glanced around as if lost. Marcus walked over to him and asked, "Can I help you, sir?"

Frank opened his notebook and started copying the names and destinations of those who had signed in on Saturday morning. He finished just as Marcus returned to the desk.

"Thanks," Frank said. "No sign of my bud's name. I *knew* that was him I saw!"

Frank's next stop was the library. He found a seat in a quiet corner and studied the list of names he had copied. There were almost as many staff members as students. He recognized a lot of the names from different classes, sports, and extracurricular activities.

If this counted as a quiet Saturday morning, Frank thought, he was glad he didn't have to deal with a busy one. The hockey, girls' basketball, and fencing teams all had had practice. The jazz combo had rehearsed. Half a dozen kids had signed in to work in the video lab. Under "Purpose of Visit," no one had written, "Telemarketing of stolen achievement test."

Frank was checking his watch when the bell rang. He gathered his stuff and left the library. He was supposed to go to lunch but went to the gym instead. As he threaded his way through the crowded corridor, he checked out backpacks. Some were orange, but none of those had a black mesh pocket.

An outfielder named Jerry came along. He stopped Frank and took his arm. "Hey," he said, "what's all this about Joe?"

"What did you hear?" Frank asked cautiously.

"Something about being kicked out for cheating on a test," Jerry replied. "The guy who told me doesn't know Joe personally. I told him it was a load of lies and he shouldn't spread nasty rumors."

"Good advice," Frank said. "What happened is, Joe was accused of something he didn't do. He's on suspension."

"No way!" Jerry exclaimed. "That's lousy."

"It sure is," Frank said. "And you can bet I'm doing all I can to clear him. Hey, listen, have you heard any talk the last few days about the SAB?"

"That state test that's coming up?" Jerry asked. "Now you mention it, yeah. They're saying there are copies for sale. Pretty raw if it's true. That could wreck the curve for the rest of us."

"Do you actually know anyone who's bought it?" Frank asked.

Jerry shook his head. "No. It's always 'I know a guy whose friend told him that he'd heard from his cousin that . . .' You know how it is."

Frank gave him a rueful smile. "Sure do," he said. "Okay, thanks. I'll tell Joe hi from you."

It was a long walk to the gym. By the time Frank got there, the bell was ringing. He went inside. Half a dozen groups were scattered around the enormous room. Some were doing warm-up exercises. Others were already practicing. As usual, the floor along the wall near the entrance was piled high with backpacks.

Frank walked slowly along the line of packs, scanning them. He paused at one that was orange with a bright blue flap, then shook his head and went on. He was nearing the far wall when he froze. His eyes widened. There on the floor, partly hidden by another pack, was an orange pack with a black mesh pocket on the front!

A nametag dangled from one of the zipper pulls. Frank squatted down to read it.

"Hey, you!" someone yelled in Frank's ear. "What do you think you're doing?"

Two hands grabbed his shoulders and pulled. He felt himself falling backward.

5 Body Check

Frank's reflexes had been sharpened by many hours of martial arts training. As the attacker pulled him backward, Frank tucked his chin into his chest, drew up his knees, and thrust himself in the direction of the motion.

His opponent, surprised by the move, let go of Frank's shoulders and took a step back.

Frank completed a swift backward somersault and sprang to his feet. Hands raised defensively, he spun around to face his attacker. He recognized him at once. It was Carl, the hockey player who had almost crashed into Callie at the lake on Sunday afternoon.

"Caught you red-handed," Carl growled. "I ought to punch you out!"

Carl's friend, Brad, joined him. "What's going on?" he asked.

"I caught this jerk trying to rip off something from your backpack," Carl announced, pointing a finger at Frank.

"Wrong," Frank said. "That pack looks like my friend Tony's. I couldn't figure out what it was doing here since he's not in school. I was trying to look at the nametag, that's all."

"Tony?" Brad repeated. "Are you talking about Tony Prito? He just got kicked out of school for lifting a test, didn't he?"

"Hey, that's right," Carl said. "And this dude's Frank Hardy. His kid brother got kicked out too. What do you want to bet he was about to put something in your backpack, to clear his brother? We ought to teach him a lesson."

Frank planted his feet and raised his arms, ready to meet their attack.

"Hold on!" someone ordered. "What's going on?"

A man with short dark hair and bushy eyebrows stepped between Frank and the two hockey players. Under his dark blue running suit, he was wearing a T-shirt from an ice hockey tournament. A silver whistle dangled from a lanyard around his neck.

"I'm Coach Dobeny," he told Frank. "Who are you, and why you are disrupting our practice?"

Frank identified himself.

45

"He's a professional snoop, him and his brother," Carl said, breaking in. "I caught him messing with Brad's backpack."

Frank repeated his explanation. "All I wanted to do was read the nametag," he finally said. "I didn't even touch the pack."

Dobeny looked over at Carl. "Do you agree with his account?" he asked.

Reluctantly Carl answered, "I guess so. But that's only because I caught him before he opened it."

"All right, I'll handle this," Dobeny said. "Carl, Brad, get back to your workout."

Before turning away, Carl gave Frank a dirty look.

"Now, Frank," Dobeny said in a low voice, "I've heard a little about you and your brother, and I've heard about what just happened to him. I don't know what you're up to—"

"I already told you," Frank said.

The coach frowned. He obviously didn't like having students talk back to him. "Let me finish. I have some good advice for you. Leave Brad Austin out of your plans. He's a key player on our team. We have the most important game of the season coming up, against New Harbor. If anybody did something that kept him from playing, I'm afraid his friends and teammates would be very unhappy. Do you hear what I'm saying? *Very* unhappy!"

Dobeny stared Frank in the eye for a moment, then spun on his heel and strode back to the waiting hockey players.

Frank left the gym. His stomach rumbled, reminding him this was his lunch period. On the way to the cafeteria, he stopped at a pay phone and called home. Joe picked up on the first ring.

"I'm glad I caught you. Any new developments?" Frank asked.

"A few," Joe replied. "I'm not sure how they fit together. First of all, I talked to Fred Adolphus, the driver for the express company. He used to go to Bayport, by the way."

"Adolphus?" Frank said. "That rings a bell. There's a girl in my class by that name. Nina Adolphus. Straight A student."

"That's right, I heard her name recently," Joe said. "You think they're related?"

"We should find out," Frank said. He made a note. "What did Adolphus tell you?"

"Get this. He left the tests sitting on the school loading dock for fifteen minutes or more, while he went hunting for the guy in charge," Joe told him.

Frank caught his breath. "Really? You mean, anybody could have snatched a copy of the test?"

"Anybody who knew they were there or happened to see them," Joe said. "Not what I'd call tight security. And there's another thing."

Frank's eyes widened as he heard about Adolphus stopping at Mr. Pizza. "What do you think?" he asked when Joe finished.

"I don't know," Joe replied. He sounded troubled. "What about you?"

"I don't know either," Frank said slowly. "But let's face it, the test *was* in Tony's backpack. And now we've come across a possible link between him and the delivery of the tests. I don't believe it for a minute. Tony's not that kind of guy. But friend or not, we've got to check it out. Luckily, it's not our only lead." He told Joe about Brad Austin and his backpack.

"Wait a minute," Joe said. "You mean, the test could have been meant for him?"

"Could be," Frank said. "He's a key player on the hockey team, with a big game coming up. How he scores on the SAB might affect his eligibility. I'll talk to people in his classes and find out how he does."

"Good idea," Joe said. "Take it easy, though. Word could get back to him that you're asking questions. I have a hunch he wouldn't like that."

"Don't worry," Frank said, a little irritated by the warning. "Now, here's another thing. There were more calls offering to sell the test on Sunday afternoon. At least one was made from a pay phone at a gas station at Franklin and Pershing. Can you check it out?"

"Sure thing. Maybe I can even manage to get a

description of the caller. I'll also go by that tutoring service. Maybe there's no connection, but it's worth a closer look."

Joe drove along Franklin Avenue, glancing at the stores he passed. They advertised auto parts, carpet remnants, stereos, and cheap furniture. None of them seemed to be selling much. A storefront lawyer, a nail salon, and a couple of takeout joints completed the scene.

Joe spotted the gas station. The pay phone was attached to the wall between the soda machine and the door to the office. He turned in and pulled up next to the pumps. After filling the van's tank, he went inside.

A tired-looking woman in jeans and a down vest stood behind the counter, filling out some forms. She took Joe's gas credit card and slid it through the reader, then handed him the slip and a ballpoint.

"Mind if I ask you a question?" Joe said as he scribbled his signature.

The woman gave him a wary look. "What about?"

"My girlfriend got a couple of crank calls over the weekend," Joe replied. "Nothing really weird, but they bothered her, you know? Well, she got the number they were coming from and asked me to check it out."

"Good for her," the woman said. "Creeps who pull stunts like that should be locked up."

"Well," Joe said, "it turns out the calls came from that pay phone outside. I was wondering if you noticed anybody making a bunch of calls on Sunday afternoon."

"Now you mention it, I did," the woman said, straightening up. "It struck me as funny, since it was freezing out there."

"Can you describe the guy?" Joe asked. He held his breath. Was this the break they needed in this case?

The woman frowned. "Well . . . not really. Sort of average height. Not particularly skinny or fat. He had the hood up on his parka, so I didn't see his face."

"Do you remember what color his parka was?" Joe asked.

"Blue," the woman said. "Sort of medium blue, lighter than navy. The reason I noticed, it was almost exactly the same color as his SUV. I had to laugh. What do you think? Did he buy the parka to match his car or the other way around?"

Joe followed up with more questions, but the woman had already told him all she could. He thanked her and went back to the van to make a note of the conversation.

The address for U-Score-Hi was in the same part of town, about half a mile away. Joe drove there and parked in front of a two-story frame building with a sagging roofline and peeling paint. A launderette occupied the first floor. The weed-choked lot next door was in use as a parking lot.

Joe found an entrance at the side, went in, and climbed a flight of squeaky stairs. The door at the top was half wood and half frosted glass. Stick-on letters spelled out "U-Score-Hi, S. Martin, Pres." He knocked and went in.

The reception room was just big enough for a secretary's desk and half a dozen scarred wooden school chairs. There was no one in sight. Through an open door on the left wall, someone called, "In here!"

Joe went over. The second room was even smaller than the first. It was furnished with a gray metal office desk and three chairs. A man of about forty, with thinning black hair and a heavy five o'clock shadow, looked up from behind the desk.

"Just put it here," he said. "Oh, sorry—I thought you were from the Chinese restaurant. I'm waiting for my lunch."

"I can come back later," Joe said.

"No, no," the man said hastily. "Come in, sit down. Business before pleasure. I'm Sal Martin, president and general director of U-Score-Hi. And you are . . ."

Joe sat in one of the chairs and said, "My name's Joe Hardy. I'm a student at Bayport High."

"And you're a little concerned about this new state test, am I right?" Martin said. "You want to make sure you do well on it."

51

"Um, yeah, it's pretty important to me," Joe said. "I'd give a lot to feel more confident."

"Joe, you have come to the right place," Martin said, pointing a forefinger in Joe's direction. "At U-Score-Hi you get guaranteed results. That's a promise."

"How does that work?" Joe asked. "We don't have a lot of time before the test."

"I know that," Martin said. "And with our twenty-first–century methods, you don't need a lot of time. What would you say to a single two-hour session?"

Joe stared at him. "Two hours? That's it?"

"And with guaranteed results," Martin told him. "You don't pass, we give your money back. Believe me, Joe, when you leave here, you know the answers. Sound good?"

"Too good to be true," Joe replied. "Er, is it very expensive? I've heard these prep courses cost a fortune."

"Some of them do," Martin said. "I call it gouging the public. Here at U-Score-Hi we've done everything we can to keep our service affordable. The total cost of the course, including materials, is only two hundred dollars, payable in two easy installments. What do you say, Joe? Are you on board?"

"I don't know," Joe said. "It sounds like what I need, but I have to think it over."

"You do that, Joe," Martin said. "But I'd better warn you. Our available spaces are filling up fast. I'd hate to have to turn you away. This is your whole future we're talking about."

"I'll keep that in mind," Joe replied. He stood up.

There was a knock on the outer door. A voice called, "Delivery."

"In here," Martin called back. He took an envelope from his desk drawer and emptied a pile of change on the desk, then started separating out the quarters. Joe stepped aside to let the delivery guy in and left.

Downstairs Joe started the van and pulled out into traffic. A moment later he stomped on the brakes. A horn blared from behind. He ignored it. He waited until traffic cleared. Then he made a quick U-turn, pulled into a parking space on the far side of the street, and turned off the engine.

Rummaging through the glove compartment, Joe found an old baseball cap. He put it on and pulled the bill low over his eyes, then settled down in his seat. He kept his eyes fixed across the street.

The reason Joe had changed his plans so suddenly was something he had spotted in the parking lot next to the U-Score-Hi offices. It was a blue SUV.

6 None of the Above

Frank carried his lunch tray over to the usual table. Callie, Iola, and Chet were already there.

"Any news?" Callie asked eagerly.

"Sort of," Frank replied. "But the most we can do right now is gather up pieces of the puzzle that we don't even know for sure all come from the same puzzle. Then we can try to fit them together to figure out what they mean."

"What about that telephone number I got from Marcy?" asked Chet. "Was that any help?"

"Joe's checking it out," Frank replied.

"Someone gave me a number for the guy who's trying to sell the test," Chet explained to Iola and Callie.

"Hey, that reminds me," Frank said. "Any of you know a skater named Brendan?"

The others shook their heads.

"Well, he told me an odd story. He's one of the people who got a call from this guy. And he said he'd buy the test. But instead of closing the deal, the guy hung up on him. What do you make of that?"

"Was this Brendan serious about buying it?" Iola asked.

Frank shrugged. "Hard to say. His story now is that he was only kidding. Why? Do you think that might have come across?"

"Could be," Iola said. "Maybe he laughed or something. Or said yes too fast. You don't come up with five hundred bucks easily."

"Good point," Frank said. "Joe's also checking out the tutoring service that's been calling people about the test. The deal they're offering sounds pretty fishy. Oh—do any of you know a girl named Nina Adolphus?"

"I do," Callie said. "From chemistry. She's really smart."

"Do you happen to know if she has an older brother?" Frank asked. Callie shook her head. "Could you find out?"

"I guess so," she said.

"What about me?" Chet said. "Do I get an assignment too?"

Frank pressed his index finger to his temple. "I'm thinking, I'm thinking," he said. "Do you know anybody on the hockey team?"

"Yeah," Chet replied. "Barry Waxman. We used to play together when we were little."

"Oh, sure, I remember him," Iola said. "He has red hair and funny ears."

"Have a talk with him. See what you can find out about a couple of hockey players, Carl Shute and Brad Austin," Frank told Chet.

"Sure. Why them?"

"Brad has a backpack that looks a lot like Tony's," Frank replied, "and the two packs were probably near each other in the gym yesterday."

"I get it," Iola said. "You figure somebody put the test in Tony's backpack, thinking it was Brad's. Right?"

Frank hesitated. Should he mention the possibility that Tony was somehow involved? So far there was no evidence to back it up.

"That's the best theory we've got so far," Frank told Iola.

"Somebody's got a real generous streak," Chet said jokingly. "Just think, the going price on those suckers is five hundred bucks. Someone must like this Brad guy a lot to give it to him like that."

"Some gift," Callie remarked. "It hasn't done a lot of good for Tony and Joe."

"It wasn't the test that did that," Chet said. "It

was Old Beady Eyes. With a big boost from everybody's favorite girl reporter."

"Speak of the devil," Iola muttered, "here she comes now."

Frank looked around. Liz Webling was marching across the cafeteria toward their table. She didn't look to either side or seem to notice anyone else. Still, Frank was sure she knew people around the room were watching and talking about her.

Liz stopped an arm's length from the table. "Frank, we need to talk," she announced.

"Sure, Liz," Frank replied. He spread his arms wide. "Here I am. Talk."

"Alone," Liz said, with steel in her voice.

Frank gestured toward his tray. "Can it wait? I'm in the middle of lunch."

"This can't wait," Liz insisted.

Callie stood up and motioned to Chet and Iola to do the same. "Excuse us," she said, giving Liz a cold look. "Frank, we'll catch you later."

The three friends picked up their trays and carried them across the room to the disposal area. Liz took Callie's seat, across the table from Frank.

"So," Frank said, after a deliberate bite of his sandwich, "what's so urgent?"

"This business with the SAB," Liz replied. "You're investigating it. Don't bother to deny it. I have witnesses."

"What makes you think I'd deny it?" Frank

asked. "My brother's been falsely accused of something and unfairly punished. Not to mention being the target of a sneak attack in the media. You bet I'm going to clear him."

"Your cases are news," Liz said. "And this one could be very big news. It could reach way beyond Bayport High School. All the way to the state level. It's an opportunity I'm not going to miss."

"Uh-huh," Frank said. He took a sip of milk.

"So here's the deal," Liz said. "Whatever you find out, I expect you to tell me first. I want an exclusive."

Frank waited for a few moments. Then he asked, "What's the rest of it?"

"I don't know what you mean," Liz said, lowering her eyes.

"Sure you do," Frank said. "You know, the part that starts off 'Or else . . .' After that show you put on last night, I can't think of one good reason I should even talk to you. But you obviously think you've got one for me. Okay, I give up. What is it?"

Liz's face reddened. Still not looking at him, she said, "If your brother's innocent, you've got no reason not to cooperate with me. So if you *don't* cooperate, that's evidence he really is involved. And that's something the public needs to know, isn't it?"

"Let me see if I've got this straight," Frank said. "Either we hand you a big story, or you trash Joe's rep even more. Is that the deal you're offering?"

"I didn't say that," Liz said.

"Oh? Good thing," Frank said. "Because that sounds an awful lot like blackmail. Does the news or Channel Sixty-one make it a practice to blackmail? If so, that's news right there."

"Hold on," Liz said, clutching the edge of the table. "I said cooperate. You share what you learn with me, I share what I learn with you. That's fair, isn't it?"

"Sure," Frank replied. "As long as both sides are willing and they put about the same amount into the pot. Is that what we're talking about here?"

Liz pushed back her chair and stood up. "This isn't getting us anywhere," she announced with a narrow-eyed stare. "Think it over, Frank. But don't take too long. I'm already working on the script for tonight's show. I haven't decided yet if you and Joe are heroes or villains. It's up to you to convince me . . . one way or the other."

Liz left. Frank sat very still and thought—not just about Liz and her "deal," but about the shape of the whole case. Job one of course was to clear Joe's name. The obvious way to do that was to find out who had taken the copy of the test. Figure out *when* and *how*, and chances were you'd know *who*.

Who had opportunity? Who had been in a position to steal the test? The truck driver, Fred, certainly. The guys in the school's receiving department too. But who else? What about Fred's stop at Mr. Pizza?

Was Tony even there at the time? He and Joe would have to pin that down.

Callie touched Frank's shoulder. "Was she awful?" she asked.

"Hmm?" Frank blinked. "Oh—Liz? About average, I'd say. For her. I even felt a little sorry for her. She's trying to play hardball, but all she's got is a Ping Pong paddle."

Callie laughed. "I *think* I know what that means. Listen, I just had a piece of luck. I spotted Nina Adolphus, so I went over and started a conversation. She must have thought it was pretty strange when I asked her if she has any brothers. It's not as if we know each other very well."

"But you did ask her, right?" Frank said. "And?"

"She has *two* brothers," Callie announced with triumph in her voice. "One's in eighth grade. The other's twenty-two. He's living at home while he works and saves up to go back to college. Nina's proud of him."

"She didn't mention his name, did she?" Frank asked.

"Not at first," Callie replied. "But I kept her talking until she did. It's Fred."

"All right!" Frank said. "Good work, Callie. Do you have a few minutes? I think we should have another talk with that guy in Receiving. Especially after what we overheard yesterday and what we've found out since."

"Sure, let's go," Callie said.

As Frank and Callie neared the door to the receiving area, it swung open. A dark-haired man in khakis came out, pushing a dolly loaded with cartons. As they stepped aside to let him by, he gave them a sharp glance.

They walked down the concrete ramp to the loading dock. Mel was working at his desk in the little glassed-in booth. He heard their footsteps and called over his shoulder, "You kids go back the way you came. You're not allowed through here."

"We came to talk to you," Frank replied.

Mel looked around, his expression hard. "You again," he growled, getting to his feet. "What do you want?"

"We're going on with our research on security procedures here at the school," Frank replied. "And we've turned up some things we don't understand."

"I told you yesterday," Mel said. "I've got nothing to say."

"It's about last Thursday afternoon," Callie said. "A very sensitive shipment came in. It was supposed to be kept under tight security. But it wasn't, was it?"

Mel's hands tightened into fists. "You have any questions, take them up with my supervisor," he said, his voice rising.

"Are you sure you want us to do that?" Frank

asked. "Do your bosses know those cartons of tests sat out on the loading dock, unwatched, for a while? I don't think so."

"Get out of here!" Mel shouted. "This area's off-limits to students. If you're not gone before I count to three, I'm calling a guard. One . . ."

"Who had access to those boxes?" Callie asked. "Just you and your assistant, right? That doesn't look good, does it?"

Mel's face reddened. The veins in his neck bulged. "You're nuts!" he declared. "You're talking access? Everybody and his brother walks through here. They use it as a shortcut. I try to stop them, but they just laugh at me. It's like they own the place. And I can't lock the door because delivery people need to get in. Now will you two get out of my face? Or do I call the guard?" He reached for the telephone on his desk.

"Okay, we're going," Frank said. "But sooner or later you're going to have to come up with some answers to our questions. Come on, Callie," he added. They turned their backs on Mel and started up the ramp.

Frank frowned. What was that rumbling sound? He peered into the shadows and gasped.

A dolly piled high with cartons blocked the top of the ramp. It started rolling down the slope toward them, gathering speed as it went.

Frank instantly scanned their surroundings. One

side of the ramp was a blank wall. On the other was a pipe railing, with a five-foot drop beyond. He and Callie didn't have enough room to get out of the way or enough time to run back down the ramp.

They were trapped!

7 A Leap in Time

"Frank, look out!" Callie screamed.

The loaded dolly raced down the ramp toward them. It was less than a dozen feet away now and picking up speed.

Frank acted so quickly, so exactly, it was as if he and Callie had rehearsed for days. He sprang to her side and grabbed her by the waist. In one smooth motion, he lifted her up and across the top of the railing.

"Get ready!" Frank shouted. He released his grip. He sensed Callie preparing to take the force of a drop from shoulder height to the floor below. He had no time to make sure she was all right, though. No time to vault the railing himself either. The dolly was about to smash into him.

Frank crouched down, then ordered his trained, powerful leg muscles to thrust him upward. An instant later the upper edge of the dolly slammed into his stomach. Frank doubled over, gasping for breath, and scrabbled to find handholds. His head and chest were on top of the cartons, his legs dangling over the front.

The careering dolly hit the bottom of the ramp, bounced, and sped across the concrete floor of the loading dock. Frank knew he had escaped only the first danger. He was still far from safe.

Gathering his strength, he hoisted his lower body up onto the top of the cartons. It felt as if he were doing a chin-up with a barbell strapped to his ankles. After what seemed forever, he managed to get his feet under him. He crouched and leaped off the back of the dolly.

Frank's feet hit the concrete hard. He fell forward onto his hands and knees. An instant later an earsplitting crash rocked the room. Frank twisted around to look. The dolly and its cargo had just smashed into the metal door of the loading dock.

"Frank! Are you hurt?" Callie ran over and helped him to his feet.

Frank's palms stung from scraping across the concrete floor, and his knees were complaining. Otherwise he was all right. "I'm okay," he said. "How about you?"

"I'm—" Callie started to speak.

Mel rushed up. His face was pale with fright. "What kind of stupid stunt was that!" he shouted. "You could have been killed!"

"Hold on," Frank barked. "Are you trying to say this was *our* fault? We didn't send that thing rolling down the ramp, but I'd like to know who did!"

Mel stared at Frank for a moment. Then he turned toward the ramp and yelled, "Ramon! *Ramon!* Get down here, right now!"

A dark-haired man in khakis hurried down the ramp. Frank recognized him. It was the man he and Callie had passed in the corridor on the way to the receiving area.

"What is it?" Ramon exclaimed in alarm. "What happened?"

Mel pointed toward the dolly. "What was that doing on the ramp with the brakes off?" he demanded.

Ramon's jaw dropped. "The brakes were on," he said. "I know I set them!"

Frank stepped over to the dolly. Each rear wheel had a foot-operated lever attached to its hub. "Down is locked, right?" he said. "These are less than halfway down. Not enough to hold it on a slope."

"It was an accident," Ramon said.

Mel gave a loud snort. "It was carelessness. And you can bet I won't forget this come evaluation time."

He turned to Frank and Callie. "As for you, I told you before. This area's off-limits to students. Now you see why. If you hadn't been hanging around, there wouldn't have been a problem. Now, will you please get out of here!"

"Gladly," Callie said. "But remember, we still intend to get answers to our questions."

Red-faced once again, Mel pointed toward the exit. "Out! Now! And don't come back!"

Frank and Callie had just enough time to get to their next classes. As they walked, they talked over what had just happened.

"An accident? I doubt it," Frank said. "A warning is more like it."

"From Ramon?" Callie said. "Or were they both in on it? Maybe Ramon was just following Mel's orders."

"Either way, the question is why," Frank said. "What are they trying to keep us from finding out?"

"That they messed up on security when the SABs were delivered," Callie said.

"But we know that already," Frank replied. "And Mel *knows* we know."

"Maybe that's what the warning means," Callie said. "Keep your mouths shut or else."

"Maybe," Frank commented. "But I can't help wondering. What if they're a lot more deeply involved than that? What if one of them stole the test?"

"Then we'd better be careful," Callie said. "Next time we might not see the dolly coming before it hits us."

Joe folded his arms across his chest and tucked his hands in his armpits. His fingers were so cold they were turning numb. His toes were already numb. Should he start the engine and turn on the heater? No, not a good idea. It would send a cloud of white condensation out from the tailpipe. Everyone on the block would see there was someone in the van and wonder why he was sitting there.

Joe's stomach rumbled. He had turned up a stale granola bar in the glove compartment, but that had been an hour earlier. If only he'd picked up something at the gas station—a box of cookies or a bag of chips. Even a pack of gum would have helped. He and Frank should equip the van with emergency rations just for situations like this.

Was this a total waste of time? Joe settled lower in his seat and rested his chin on his chest. The blue SUV still sat in the same place in the parking lot across the street. For all Joe knew, it might be there for the next week. Or month.

Joe realized there was a lot he didn't know. He didn't even know if this was the blue SUV the woman at the gas station had described. He didn't know if it belonged to Sal Martin. He didn't know if Martin had any connection to the stolen test in Tony's backpack.

Without facts, all he could do was pay attention to his instinct. And for now his instinct told him to watch the SUV and follow it if it went anywhere.

Across the street the side door to the tutoring services swung open. Joe sat up eagerly. Sal Martin came out. He was wearing a black leather jacket and a gray hat. He stopped on the sidewalk and glanced around. As he looked toward the van, Joe ducked to hide his face behind the bill of his cap.

Martin walked to the parking lot beside the building and climbed into the blue SUV.

Ha! Joe said to himself. Gotcha! He reached for the ignition key.

Martin pulled out of the lot and turned right. Joe started the van, waited a few moments, and made a U-turn onto his tail. He left a space of a little less than a block between the two vehicles, figuring that should be close enough to keep tabs on Martin, but far enough to make it less likely he would be noticed.

Martin turned right at the next corner, then left three blocks later. Half a mile farther along, he drove into the parking lot of a supermarket. Joe made a face. Was this a simple shopping trip?

No. Just as Joe entered the parking lot, he saw Martin coming *out*. What was this? A change of plans? Or maybe a tactic to check for a tail? If so, Joe could only hope he hadn't been spotted.

By the time Joe turned around and left the lot,

Martin was almost two blocks away. Joe sped up to narrow the gap, then decided to fall back again. The SUV was so tall that it showed over the roofs of the cars in between. That meant Joe could follow it from a greater distance.

At the next traffic light Martin turned left again, then made still another left three blocks later. They were back on Markham Street now, going the way they had come. Martin had just made a big, point-less loop. Joe was convinced that he realized he had a tail.

As they approached the block where Martin's office was located, Joe was half expecting to see the SUV pull back into the lot and park. It wouldn't have surprised him if Martin had gotten out of the car and thumbed his nose at Joe!

But Martin didn't even slow down as he passed the lot. He continued up the street and turned right. They were just a few blocks from the gas station. Was Martin heading there to make more phone calls?

Another guess shot down. The blue SUV contin-ued on for another mile or so. Then it turned into the lot of a block-long strip mall and parked in front of a storefront with a big For Lease sign in the win-dow. Was this another tactic to check for a tail?

Joe drove past and entered the lot at the far end of the block. He parked with his front wheels against a curb-high divider thirty yards down from

Martin. He adjusted his mirror. This allowed him to keep an eye on the SUV without being obvious.

For several minutes nothing happened. Then a car drove in and parked in the slot to the right of Martin's. Joe grabbed his notebook. The car was a four-door sedan, about ten years old, and painted a rusty brown. From this angle he couldn't read the license plate. He did see something else that made him think, however. In the lower right corner of the rear window was a Bayport High School decal.

Joe watched Martin shift over to the passenger seat of the SUV and roll down the window. He and the driver of the brown car talked for several minutes. Joe wished he had brought a parabolic mike and sensitive recording equipment with him.

Martin rolled his window back up. A puff of black smoke announced that the brown car had just started up again. As it backed out of the space, Joe craned his neck to get a glimpse of the driver or the license number. No such luck. Should he try to follow the car or stay on Martin's tail?

While Joe tried to decide on his next move, he felt a sudden jolt that whipped his head back.

"What—" he exclaimed.

Joe turned to look past the high back of the driver's seat. All he could see through the van's rear window was the hood and windshield of an oversize black pickup truck that had just bumped into him. An accident? Not likely.

Glancing quickly from one side mirror to the other, Joe saw two burly guys climb down from the pickup. They were dressed alike, in brown bomber jackets and dark caps. The one on the driver's side held a pipe wrench in his hand. The other carried an aluminum baseball bat.

As Joe reached for the ignition key, he heard a crash. A window on the right side of the van was shattered.

8 Slip-sliding Away

Joe turned the key in the ignition, and the van's engine screamed to life. He made a lightning decision. The black pickup kept him from backing up. In front the van's wheels were blocked by the divider. But the van had a few unusual features. One of the neatest was a heavy-duty transmission with a two-speed rear axle.

Joe grabbed the small lever next to the gearshift and shoved it into low. A movement to the left caught his eye. The thug with the wrench was only inches away, on the other side of the glass. With a snarl he lifted his weapon to smash Joe's window. Joe grasped the door handle, cranked the steering wheel to the left, and stomped on the gas pedal.

The van bucked. For a heart-stopping instant,

Joe was sure the engine would stall, leaving him helpless. Then, suddenly, the front wheels bounced up over the divider. The van leaped forward and swerved. As it did, Joe shoved open his door. It slammed into the thug, who stumbled backward and fell. The wrench went spinning through the air and crashed down on a parked car twenty feet away.

The rear tires squealed as the van fishtailed. Joe risked a quick glance in his right mirror. The second thug, the one who had smashed the window, was backing away with terror on his face, his bat forgotten on the pavement.

With a grim smile, Joe turned his attention back to his driving. He raced along to the end of the parking lot, then braked. Which way now?

Joe checked both ways. Down the block, the blue SUV zoomed back in his direction. At the same time, the black pickup came speeding through the parking lot. In another moment he would be trapped between them.

Joe clamped his jaw tight and took a deep breath. With odds like these, his only hope was to do something totally unexpected. He tightened his grip on the steering wheel and turned right, toward the approaching SUV. He pressed the accelerator to the floor. Behind him, the pickup followed. It accelerated until it was only a foot from his rear bumper.

Less than half a block separated Joe from Martin's SUV. He carefully watched the quickly narrowing gap. In his mind he counted down: three . . . two . . . one . . .

Now!

At the last possible moment Joe swung the wheel hard to the left and sped onto the road. His tires screamed in protest. The van crossed directly in front of the speeding SUV. Taken by surprise, Martin swerved to his left, right into the path of the pickup truck. Horns blared. The two vehicles sideswiped each other and stopped in a tangle of tortured metal.

Joe quickly steered the van back into its proper lane. He stopped down the block long enough to see Martin and the two thugs climb out of the wreckage unhurt. Once his heart rate had returned to normal, he drove to an auto glass shop to get the shattered window replaced. He had a wicked impulse to send the bill to Sal Martin.

By now it was after three o'clock. Joe went by Bayport High and picked up a packet of assignments from Sheldrake's secretary. As he left, he realized that he still hadn't had lunch. He decided to combine pleasure with business. He drove to Mr. Pizza, parked down the block, and went inside. Dave, who was behind the counter, recognized Joe.

"Hey," he said, "how's it going? You want a slice?"

"Make it two slices, with mushrooms," Joe replied.

"You got it," Dave said. He sprinkled mushrooms on the two slices of pizza and slid them into the oven.

"Say, Dave," Joe said, "did you work last Thursday?"

"Sure. I'm here Monday through Friday," Dave replied. "Why?"

"Did you happen to notice a guy named Fred who's a driver for the express company?" Joe asked. "I heard he stopped by about this time."

"Yeah, I know who you mean," Dave said. "He was a couple of years ahead of me in high school. Thursday . . . Oh, right. I remember. Yeah, he dropped in for a slice. With anchovies, I think."

"You've got some memory," Joe said admiringly.

Dave shrugged. "Well, the thing is, his truck blocked my view of the spot where Tony usually parks. And I kept looking out the window because Tony was late. Tony's hardly ever late. That's why I remember about Fred."

"Do you know, was Fred still here when Tony showed up?" Joe asked.

"Hmm. . . . Matter of fact, he was," Dave said. "I can just see Tony coming around from in back of that big van. He looked pretty frazzled, on account of being late, I guess."

Dave took the hot slices of pizza from the oven. Joe got a can of cola from the cooler and sat down at the nearest table. He was halfway through his second slice when Tony came in the door.

"Hi," Tony said, dropping into the seat across from Joe. "I saw the van. I figured it was you. I was going to call you later."

Joe studied Tony's face. He had dark shadows under his eyes. He looked as if he hadn't slept in days. "Are you okay?" Joe asked.

"I've been better," Tony replied. He leaned forward and lowered his voice. "I got cornered by old man Sheldrake when I went by school to get my homework."

"What did he say?" Joe asked.

"The usual garbage," Tony said. "Who gave me the test, who did I show it to, what was your role in this. He mentioned Frank, too. I don't know why."

"He must be feeling some heat," Joe said. "The only evidence he has against us is the fact that you found the test in your pack."

"I got the feeling he'd like to hush the whole thing up," Tony said. "He warned me twice not to talk to anybody about it."

"Well, sure," Joe said. "If word gets around that Bayport students are cheating on the SAB, it could be really bad for the school. You remember what Callie said the other day? We could lose state aid and even be kicked out of tournaments."

"Compared to what they're doing to us, that doesn't sound like such a big deal," Tony said bitterly. He stood up. "I'd better start earning my pay here. I'll call you when I get home tonight."

* * *

Joe was in the kitchen, topping off his pizza lunch with a slice of Aunt Gertrude's apricot tart, when Frank and Chet came in.

"You won't believe what I've got to tell you!" Frank exclaimed. "What a day."

"I bet mine tops yours," Joe replied.

"Oh, yeah? Did anybody try to run you over?" Frank demanded.

"More or less," Joe told him.

"But not with a dolly load of school supplies," Frank said.

"You got me there," Joe said with a grin.

"So what happened to you?" Chet asked Joe.

Joe looked at Frank. "Tell your friend that I am not allowed to communicate with him," he said, straight-faced. "The school administration is worried I might pass along the secret blueprints for the navy's nuclear apple polisher."

"Sorry, Joe, I forgot," Chet said. "Oops! I mean, Frank, pass it on that I'm sorry."

"He's sorry," Frank told Joe. "Is that the last of the apricot tart?"

"More in the fridge," Joe said.

After a large slice of tart and a glass of milk, Chet went home. Joe and Frank filled each other in on what had happened and what they had learned. It took awhile.

Finally Frank leaned back and said, "There's a lot

to keep track of." He took a sheet of paper from his loose-leaf notebook and wrote "SAB" at the top.

For the next half hour the Hardys discussed the case so far while Frank took notes. When they finished, Frank looked over the page and said, "You know something funny?"

"Sure. Your face," Joe said.

Frank ignored the crack. "All these rumors and phone calls about selling the test," he said slowly. "But so far only one copy of the test has turned up. The one in Tony's pack."

"The only one we *know* about," Joe said. "If you'd just paid a lot of money for a stolen test, would you go waving it around?"

"Do we know if more than one copy was stolen?" Frank wondered. "The school officials must have counted the rest of them to find out."

"It doesn't matter," Joe said. "I could run off a hundred photocopies before you turned around. I could even scan it and post it on the Internet."

"But the one in Tony's pack was still sealed," Frank said.

"As Old Beady Eyes said, these things can be resealed," Joe retorted. "What's your point?"

"I'm not sure," Frank said uneasily. "It seems funny to me, that's all."

At seven o'clock Frank and Joe once more joined their mother and aunt in front of the television. This time Liz had the lead story. The visuals included a shot of Bayport High School from the street, a student leaning over a test form, and a question mark that expanded to fill the screen. After a couple of minutes another reporter came on to talk about the town planning commission. Frank reached for the control and switched off the TV.

"Do you realize what she just said?" Frank asked.

"I didn't hear her say much of anything," Joe replied.

"That's exactly right," Frank said. "Lots of dark hints, but not one single piece of hard information. No wonder she wants us to share what we've learned. She doesn't know a thing."

"Maybe she's been asked to keep quiet about what she knows," Mrs. Hardy said. "I must say, when I spoke to Mr. Chambers this morning, I got the strong impression he wished this whole matter would quietly go away."

"Then why did he let Sheldrake suspend me and Tony?" Joe demanded.

"Naturally he wouldn't criticize his staff to an outsider," Mrs. Hardy said. "But if he had been on hand when this came up, I think he would have handled it very differently. I gave him a lot to think about. I hope it has a good effect."

The phone rang. It was Fenton Hardy, calling from Washington. Frank and Joe got on separate extensions. After they had filled him in on the case so far, he said, "The name Sal Martin rings some kind of bell with me. I suggest you check my files. You may find some information on him."

"We were planning to ask if we could do that," Frank said. "Thanks, Dad."

After handing the phone to their mother, Frank and Joe went into their father's office and booted up the computer. Joe sat at the keyboard. Frank looked over his shoulder.

"Okay, I've given the password and accessed the database," Joe announced after a few moments. "Let's do a search for Sal Martin."

Nothing came up.

"That's odd," Frank said. "Dad thought he knew the name. He isn't usually wrong about things like this."

"Maybe he was thinking of someone else with a similar name," Joe commented.

"Or maybe Sal Martin isn't our dude's real name," Frank said. "I know, let's do a wild card search. Try 'S. Mart.'"

Joe typed it in and pushed enter. Immediately a record came on the screen.

"'Salvador Martinez,'" Joe read. "'Low-level links to organized crime, involved with gangs in trucking and refuse hauling.' Does that sound like the same guy to you?"

"Look," Frank said, pointing to the screen. "He was charged with fraud in connection with commercial driver's license exams. That's him all right.

And after today we know he has some goons for friends. My question is, Does he have contacts at the express company who might be willing to steal a copy of the SAB for him?"

Joe spent the rest of the evening doing homework. It was hard to concentrate on the history readings when his mind kept going over the day's events. Finally he decided to go to bed. The day's excitement had been more of a strain than he'd realized. He was asleep practically the moment his head hit the pillow.

Much later he woke up. His alarm clock read 2:42. He lay in bed wondering what had disturbed him. He had a faint recollection of a noise from outside. After listening for a couple of minutes to the silence, he got up and padded over to the window. It was a cold, crisp night. In the clear air the stars looked close enough to touch.

Joe peered down. A car parked in front of the house started up. A very late visitor to one of the neighbors? It looked that way. Maybe it was the sound of the car door closing that had awakened him. The car pulled away with its headlights still off. Joe stayed at the window a few moments longer, then went back to bed.

"Hurry it up, Frank," Joe called from the window of the van. "We won't have time to drop by Tony's unless we leave right now. You don't want to be late for school."

"Coming, coming," Frank replied. He came out the back door, clutching his parka and backpack in his arms.

As soon as Frank sat down and fastened his seat belt, Joe started backing down the driveway. When he neared the street, he noticed a garbage truck coming up the block. He put his foot on the brake pedal. To his surprise, the van kept moving down the drive.

"Uh-oh," Joe muttered. "Houston, we have a problem."

He pressed harder on the brake pedal. He could tell that the brakes were stopping the wheels just the way they were supposed to. The problem was with the tires. They had no grip at all. It felt as if they were slipping on glare ice. The van slid faster toward the street, totally out of control.

Joe stole a quick glance over his shoulder. The garbage truck was only a couple of dozen yards away and approaching fast. The van was going to slide directly into its path, and Joe didn't know how to stop it.

"Brace yourself!" Joe shouted to Frank. "We're going to crash!"

9 On Ice

Frank felt the van start to skid even before Joe's shout. He clasped the armrests of his seat and tried to make his body go limp.

Joe was pumping the brake pedal, giving it short pushes, then letting up on it. At the same time he moved the steering wheel gently back and forth, feeling for any hint of traction.

Whether because of something Joe did or through some peculiar law of physics, the van slowly began to revolve in a clockwise direction. It kept on sliding down the driveway, but now Frank's side was closer to the street than Joe's.

The rear wheel on Joe's side slid off the driveway onto the lawn. It gouged through the thin layer of snow and the grass into the dirt. The effect was like throwing out an anchor. That corner of the van stopped moving, while the rest spun dizzily around it. A moment later the van rocked to a stop. It was resting entirely on the lawn, with the front end facing the street. The men in the garbage truck stared at the van as they roared past.

Frank took a deep breath. "Give me some warning the next time you try that," he said.

"Are you kidding?" Joe said indignantly. "Oh. Right. You *are* kidding."

"What happened?" Frank asked.

Joe shook his head. "Beats me," he said. He opened his door and climbed down. His feet shot out from under him. He clutched the van door just in time to avoid a nasty spill.

"Ice!" Joe said unbelievingly. "This whole part of the driveway is iced over."

Frank got out and walked around the van. Joe was right. For the last stretch of driveway, clear across the sidewalk to the street, the concrete glittered with a thin layer of ice.

"Weird!" Frank exclaimed. "We haven't had any snow or sleet for days. And I know the driveway was clear and dry yesterday."

"Frank, hold it," Joe said. "Something woke me in the middle of the night. When I looked out, I saw a car pull away. I didn't think anything about it then. But now . . ."

"I think you've got it," Frank said somberly.

"What a perfect booby trap! All you'd need would be a couple of five-gallon jerricans of water and a nice cold night. And I don't think our driveway got picked at random. Someone's mad at us . . . someone with a really nasty imagination."

"Sal Martin," Joe said. "I just remembered that when I went up to his office, I gave him my real name. What a bonehead move!"

"You've been smarter," Frank told him. "But from what you've told me about Martin, this isn't his style. Too indirect. He sounds like the kind who'd send some of his muscle to break our knees."

Frank walked beside the driveway to beyond the icy patch. Crossing the drive, he squatted down to get a more oblique view of the snow on that side. There were plenty of footprints, but they crossed and recrossed each other so much they were unreadable.

There was one exception. One of the intruders must have lost his balance and stepped into a deeper patch of snow.

Frank studied the print with growing excitement. First, it was big, at least a size twelve. Better still, in the instep area the sole had stamped into the snow a pattern of wheels with an inset design.

Frank took out his notebook and made a sketch of the pattern. How many running shoes had that particular design on the bottom?

"Did you find something?" Joe asked, kneeling next to him.

Frank showed Joe the pattern in the snow. "Now all we have to do," he said, "is go around making people show us the bottoms of their shoes."

"Funny," Joe said. "Frank, look over there."

Frank looked. Joe was pointing to a rectangular area where the snow was pressed down. It was about six inches wide by a foot and a half long.

"How about that!" Frank said. "I bet that was made by a steel jerrican. You know, what the army used to use for extra fuel. These days most people use those round red gas cans instead. They're lighter and easier to carry."

"Terrific," Joe said, straightening up. "So now we know. Our driveway got iced by Bigfoot driving an army surplus Jeep!"

Frank ran back to the house to leave a note warning his mother about the ice. Then he and Joe got back into the van. Joe carefully maneuvered down across the grass and into the street.

"Do we still go by Tony's?" Joe asked. "Or straight to school?"

Frank looked at his watch. He was astonished to see that the skid and its aftermath had cost them less than ten minutes. "Tony's," he replied. "We'll try to keep it short."

Tony opened his front door as they pulled into his driveway. "I thought you weren't coming," he said once they were inside. "You want something to drink? Coffee, milk, juice?"

"Sure," Frank said. "Milk for me."

"I'll have some OJ," Joe said.

The Hardys followed Tony to the kitchen and sat down in the breakfast nook overlooking the backyard. It was a sunny, comfortable spot. Frank saw Tony's backpack in the corner.

Tony poured the milk and juice and brought the glasses to the table. "Dave said you were asking about some delivery guy," he said to Joe. "Is that a lead?"

"Sort of," Joe said. "The driver who delivered the tests to the school on Thursday stopped by Mr. Pizza on the way. His name's Fred Adolphus."

Tony wrinkled his forehead. "I think I know who you mean. But what makes that a clue?"

Joe gave Frank a pleading look.

"Just that the tests were sitting out in the truck while Fred was having a slice of pizza," Frank said. "If he left the truck unlocked, anybody could have sneaked in and taken one of them."

"I guess so," Tony said slowly. "But they'd have to know the tests were in there. And they'd have to *want* to steal one. That sounds like we're looking for somebody who goes to our school."

"Could be," Frank said. "It turns out Fred's sister is in my class."

Tony ignored that. "Joe?" he said. "Listen, how come you asked Dave about what time I got to work on Thursday?"

Joe shifted uncomfortably on his seat. "The express company truck stopped at Mr. Pizza about the time you started work," he said. "Coincidence, that's all."

"Coincidence? Give me a break!" Tony said, jumping to his feet. "You guys think *I* stole that test, and that's why it was in my backpack!"

"We don't think that," Joe said. "No way. We know you better than that. But on a case you have to check out all the possibilities."

"Look at it like this," Frank added. "You and the truck and the tests were all in the same place at the same time. And you said it yourself: The test *was* in your backpack. You want us to make believe none of that's so?"

"In another minute," Tony said grimly, "I'm going to start believing *you* put the test in my pack, so you could pin it on me and build up your reps as hotshot detectives."

"Come on," Joe said. "You know—"

Tony interrupted. "What do I know? I thought I knew who my friends were. Some friends. Get out of my house, and never come back!"

Frank felt terrible. He glanced over at Joe, who looked stricken. What now? Trying to explain to Tony might just stir him up worse. It would be better to give him some time to cool off.

"I'll call you later," Joe said as the Hardys left the house.

"Don't bother," Tony retorted. He slammed the door.

Frank and Joe were subdued on the drive from Tony's house to school. When they turned onto the street that led to the front entrance, Joe said, "Hey, look. There's Callie and Iola. I know I'm not supposed to talk to them, but Old Beady Eyes didn't tell me I couldn't be in the same place."

Joe swerved over to the curb and tooted the horn. The girls noticed them. Frank pushed the rear door open, and the girls climbed in.

"Oh, it's nice and warm in here," Iola said, hugging herself.

"Good thing," Frank remarked. "Joe and I just got the cold shoulder big time." He recounted their exchange with Tony.

"I don't blame Tony one bit," Callie said. "If I found out you suspected *me* of a crime, I'd want to hit you with a chair!"

"We don't suspect him," Joe told her. "We want to eliminate him as a suspect."

"Yeah, right," Iola said sarcastically. "If you didn't think he was a suspect, why would you *need* to eliminate him?"

"What's the case against Tony?" Callie demanded. "Let's take a look at it."

"Well," Frank said, "he showed up late for work last Thursday, the same day the truck carrying the tests was in the Mr. Pizza parking lot. Was he late because he was busy taking a copy of the test from the truck?"

Callie gave a snort. "Maybe. Or maybe he was late because he got a call from the White House asking him to be on the Supreme Court! Look, did Tony *know* the truck would be there? Or that the tests would be on it? Or are you saying he checks out every truck that parks there just in case there's something on board he can steal?"

"Of course not," Joe said in a shocked voice. "Tony's not that kind of guy."

"Then why act as if he is?" Iola replied. "As far as I can see, the only hard fact against Tony is that the test was in his pack. But if *he* stole it, why would he pull it out in the middle of school and show it to you? It makes no sense!"

"Think how he must be feeling," Callie added. "First he's accused of something he didn't do and suspended from school. Then two of his best friends start treating him like a suspect."

By now Frank was starting to feel a bit picked on himself. Looking for suspects and building cases against them were what detectives did. It wasn't his fault that one of the suspects was a friend of his. *Someone* had stolen that test, and whoever it was deserved to be exposed. If nothing else, pointing out the guilty party would lift the cloud of suspicion from those who were innocent.

"Okay, you've got a point," Joe told Callie and

Iola. "The way you put it, maybe we went a little too far in checking out Tony. Maybe we ought to let him know that. If he'll talk to us at all."

Callie's reproachful gaze made Frank uncomfortable. He looked away. By now their combined breaths had misted up the van's windows. The sidewalk outside was only a hazy pattern of light and dark.

Frank frowned. From down the block a clump of dark forms moved in their direction. He sensed something purposeful, even ominous about the way they were moving. With the back of his glove, he rubbed a clear patch on the windshield.

"Joe?" he said in a quiet but intense tone. "We've got trouble."

Four guys came striding up the sidewalk toward the van. They were wearing identical dark warm-up jackets, and their faces were hidden by hockey masks. Each of them carried a hockey stick with the blade upward, ready to be used as a club.

"Let's get out of here!" Iola exclaimed.

Frank and Joe reached for their door handles at the same moment.

"We can't do that," Joe said.

"If we run away now," Frank said, "no one will ever take us seriously again."

He and Joe flung their doors open and jumped out onto the pavement. Shoulder to shoulder, with empty hands, they faced the raised sticks of their four opponents.

10 Face-off

Frank looked straight at the tallest of the four masked figures, who was half a step in front of the others.

"Okay, guys, easy," he said in a mild but firm tone. "We're not looking for any trouble."

"You've been hassling our buddies," the tall guy muttered. "We're going to teach you to leave them alone."

"We're not hassling anybody," Joe declared. "As for your buddies, whoever they are, why don't they speak for themselves?"

The rear door of the van swung open. Callie and Iola jumped out and stood next to Frank and Joe.

"What's the matter with you?" Callie demanded. Her face was pale, but there was a determined set to her jaw. "You're acting like idiots. Don't you know you can get kicked out of school for this?"

"Maybe that's why they're too scared to show their faces," Iola said loudly.

"You girls get out of our way," one of the guys growled. "If you don't, you could get hurt."

"He's right," Joe said softly. "Stand aside. We'll handle this."

Callie held up a cell phone. "I phoned the security desk at school," she announced. "They're calling the cops. If you don't beat it, you're toast."

"We've got enough time to do what we came to do," the tall guy said. Grasping his stick in both hands, he raised it over his head and rushed at Frank.

At the last moment Frank dropped to one knee. Reaching forward, he grasped the lower end of the hockey stick and gave it a hard push to the left. The leverage he gained forced his attacker's hands to cross his chest in opposite directions. His grip loosened.

Still pushing on the stick, Frank thrust his shoulder hard into the guy's midsection. Using his leg muscles, he pressed up and back. His attacker went flying. He landed flat on his back on the pavement and lay stunned. Frank held on to his hockey stick.

"Get them!" somebody shouted. The other three guys charged. Joe grappled with the first one. Against the other two, Frank used a combination of moves from tai chi. The hockey stick became a blur, blocking and striking in swirling patterns that kept his opponents confused and off guard.

One aimed a blow at Frank's face. Frank blocked it with the shaft of his stick. Then, like lightning, he slid his hands down to the wrapped handle and swung the stick like a scythe at his attacker's ankles. Intimidated, the guy jumped back, tripped, and fell.

Frank was turning to confront his other opponent when something hit him hard at the base of his skull. Dazed, he staggered forward. Through a haze, he saw one of the masked figures aim a powerful blow in the direction of his head. He told himself to duck, but his muscles were slow to obey. He clamped his jaw and braced for the blow.

It did not come. Still in a posture of defense, Frank heard someone say, "Break it up, *now!* Get out of here!"

Amazingly the four attackers obeyed. They set off at a run. Once they were far enough away to be unrecognizable, they pulled off their masks.

Frank straightened up and looked around. A man in a blue parka stood there scowling at him and Joe. Frank remembered his face. He was the assistant hockey coach, Mr. Dobeny.

"You boys are asking for big trouble," Dobeny announced.

Joe rubbed his left shoulder. "What do you call this," he asked, "a tea party?"

Callie took Frank's arm. "Are you all right?" she asked. "That creep was so sneaky, hitting you from behind like that."

Frank gingerly touched the back of his neck. The pain came and went in rhythm with his pulse. "A few minutes under a hot shower should take care of it," he said. He hoped he was right.

"I'm worried," Dobeny said. "For you and for my players. Feelings are running very high. I do not want to see the entire hockey squad suspended for fighting. We have the most important game of the season coming up."

"Then tell your players not to start fights," Iola said angrily. "This whole thing was their fault!"

"They're upset," Dobeny replied. "They think you're plotting to get our star player, Brad Austin, suspended for cheating. There are even rumors that you've been bribed by New Harbor fans to make sure Bayport loses."

"That's ridiculous," Joe proclaimed. "We've got nothing against the hockey team. Or at least we didn't before this morning. We just want to find out who stole a copy of the SAB. If somebody on the hockey team is involved, tough. But we're not after anybody in particular."

"Oh, I understand that," Dobeny said. "And I believe you're sincere. But it's a hard case to sell. Until you unmask the real thief, the suspicion and anger are bound to keep growing. How far along is your investigation? Are you getting close to an answer?"

Before Frank or Joe could respond, two patrol cars pulled up. A woman officer wearing sergeant's stripes got out of the lead car and came over to them. The name on her tag was Esmerian.

"We had a report of an altercation here," Sergeant Esmerian said, looking around the group.

"I'm a staff member at the high school, Officer," Dobeny said, and showed his ID card.

The sergeant pulled a notebook from her back pocket and opened it. After taking down everyone's name, she asked, "What was the nature of the problem here?"

Iola spoke up. "Four creeps attacked us with hockey sticks," she said.

"That's right," Callie said. "I'm the one who called school security and told them to call you."

Sergeant Esmerian turned to Frank. "Do you confirm that?"

Frank hesitated. Stories about a violent attack right down the street from the school would be terrible for Bayport's reputation. "Some guys picked a quarrel with us, yes," he said, "but you can see for yourself it's over. Everything's under control."

"I think this should be reported," Dobeny said, overruling Frank. "Incidents like this shouldn't be swept under the rug."

"I'll certainly file a report, sir," the police sergeant

said. "That's standard procedure. But I'll need to get some additional details. . . ."

For the next few minutes she asked them questions about the incident. They all denied knowing who any of the attackers were. Finally she closed her notebook.

Iola looked at her watch and groaned. "We're already way late for school," she said. "Can we go now? Please?"

"Certainly," the sergeant replied. "I appreciate your cooperation."

"I'll write an excuse for you to give to your teachers," Dobeny said as the police drove off. He took a memo pad from the pocket of his parka and scribbled, then handed each of them a slip.

"I'll call you at home," Frank told Joe hastily. He and the girls rushed off to class, leaving Joe on the sidewalk next to the van.

Frank's first-period teacher, Mr. Lee, was peeved to see him walk in halfway through a free-writing exercise. He beckoned him up to the desk. Frank explained and showed the note from Dobeny.

"Hmph," Mr. Lee murmured. "Maybe you should reserve your detective endeavors for summer vacations. Okay, take your seat."

When class ended, Chet caught up to Frank in the corridor. "What made you so late?" he asked. "Did something happen?"

"Did it!" Frank gave him a quick overview of his morning so far.

Chet's eyes opened wider and wider. "Four guys in hockey masks." He gasped. "I wish I'd been there to help. Oh, listen, speaking of hockey, I talked to my friend Barry, who's on the team. I asked him about Brad Austin and Carl Shute."

"What did you find out?" Frank asked.

"In a word, Brad's a gem and Carl's a jerk," Chet reported. "It's a mystery to Barry why they're friends. He thinks maybe Carl puts a lot of work into keeping tight with Brad. He also said Carl has a mean streak a yard wide. Even the other guys on the team stay out of his way."

"What size shoe does Carl wear?" Frank said, thinking of the footprint in the snow by his driveway.

Chet gave him a puzzled look.

"Never mind, just an in-joke." Frank then went on. "I wish I'd checked out the shoes of those guys who jumped us. I guess I was too busy watching their hockey sticks to notice."

Joe watched Frank hurry away with Callie and Iola. He felt like the only kid on the block who hadn't been asked to a birthday party. How long was this dumb suspension going to last? Until he and Frank solved the case? Then that had better be soon!

As he drove away from the school, Joe thought about the different strands of the investigation. Were there any loose ends he could try to tie up? After listening to Callie and Iola, he had pretty much crossed Tony off his list of suspects.

But what about Fred Adolphus? He had a possible motive: to help his kid sister win a scholarship. He'd certainly had a perfect opportunity while the cartons of tests were in his truck.

At the next intersection Joe turned in the direction of the express company terminal. When he got there, all the loading slots were full. One of the parked trucks was Fred's. Joe stopped on the street half a block away and settled down to wait. Twenty minutes later he saw Fred climb into his truck and drive away. He followed at a careful distance.

Fred's first stop was a camera store. Joe watched him take a stack of boxes from the back of the truck, shove the door closed with his hip, and go inside. Joe waited a moment. Then he left the van and walked quickly to the rear of the truck. He reached for the handle and turned it. As he expected, he heard the latch click. The door started to swing open.

"Oh, no, you don't!"

Joe felt someone grab his coat by the collar and jerk it downward. In an instant the sleeves had pinned his elbows to his sides. He was trapped!

11 Sealed for Your Safety

In his martial arts class Joe had learned a counter-move to this hold. It involved dropping to the ground and kicking up and backward. He decided not to use it. If possible, he wanted to avoid a fight with Fred. As a sign of that, he held himself still and allowed Fred to turn him around.

"You!" Fred exclaimed. "I thought so. Is pilfering part of your term paper?"

"I didn't take anything," Joe said.

"That's right," Fred retorted. "Because I didn't give you time. You broke into my truck, though. That's a crime."

"It was unlocked," Joe said. "That's why I tried the handle. I wanted to check if you'd locked it. Do you always leave your truck unlocked when you make a delivery?"

"We're talking about you, not me," Fred said. He gave Joe a dirty look, but he released his grip.

"I'm not a thief," Joe said, tugging his jacket back into place. "I'm a detective. Somebody stole a copy of the test you delivered to Bayport High School last week. I want to find out who."

"I know, I know," Fred said. "I mentioned your name to my kid sister last night. She's a senior at Bayport High. She told me about you and your brother. I had a hunch you'd come snooping around again. What I want to know is, why me?"

Joe decided to try shock tactics. "You had access to that test," he said, "and your sister wants to ace it."

For a long moment Fred stared at Joe. Then he dropped his shoulder and aimed a hard left at Joe's midsection. Joe saw it coming. He bobbed to the left, caught Fred's wrist, and twisted his arm into a hammerlock.

"Take it easy," Joe said softly into Fred's ear. "People are starting to look. You don't want a scene, do you?"

"Let me go," Fred yelped.

"Okay, but no more punches." Joe released his arm and took a quick step backward, just in case.

Fred glared at him. "You take back what you said about my sister!"

Joe spread his hands. "Look, I don't even know

your sister," he said. "I know she's a top student, and I heard a big college scholarship may be riding on her SAB score. And you had a better chance to take a copy of it than just about anybody. Is it my fault if that seems to add up?"

"Nina's never cheated in her life," Fred said. "She doesn't need to start now either. Besides, those cartons of tests were sealed with special security tape. Anybody monkeys with them, the tape changes color. The guy in Receiving would have noticed. He never would have signed for them."

Joe gaped. "Are you sure of that?" he demanded.

"Of course I am," Fred replied. "I checked every carton when I loaded it on the truck and again when I off-loaded them at the high school."

"I hope you're telling the truth," Joe said.

"You don't have to take my word for it," Fred declared. "Ask Mel, in Receiving. He'll tell you the same. There's no way anybody could get into those cartons without the whole world knowing."

Frank met Iola outside the library after third period.

"I called that tutoring service, the way you asked," Iola reported. "A man named Martin answered the phone. I said I was interested in their prep course for the State Achievement Battery."

"And?" Frank asked. "What did he say?"

"As soon as I said I was a student at Bayport High, he cut me off," Iola said. "He said they aren't going to offer that course after all. Something about technical difficulties. Then he hung up. I call that rude."

"I call that very interesting," Frank said. "You don't think he suspected anything about your call, do you?"

"I'm sure he didn't," Iola asserted. "I'm a pretty good actress. Besides, he sounded really sorry he couldn't take my money."

"So," Frank said musingly, "after all those phone calls to sign people up, at two hundred bucks apiece, he's calling it off. You know how I read that? If he isn't selling his so-called guaranteed results, it's because he doesn't have them to sell."

"What does that mean?" Iola asked, puzzled.

"My theory is, U-Score-Hi prepares people for tests by telling them the answers ahead of time," Frank replied. "But if you don't have the answers, you can't give them out. The way it looks to me, Martin expected to get a copy of the test somehow, so he could work out the answers and sell them. But his deal fell through. That was the technical difficulty he told you about."

"I wonder how he planned to get the test," Iola said.

"And I wonder why his plan didn't work," Frank said. Then he added, "Uh-oh."

Liz Webling marched up to them and said, "Frank, we need to talk."

Iola looked at Frank and rolled her eyes. "I was just leaving," she said.

Liz watched Iola walk away, then turned back to Frank. "I have a hot new lead in the stolen test story," she announced.

"Congratulations," Frank said dryly.

"According to my source," Liz went on, "the theft is connected to the ice hockey team."

Frank tried to keep himself from showing any reaction to this. He obviously didn't succeed.

Liz, alert, noticed. "You're following that trail too, aren't you?" she said. "How far along are you?"

"You know I can't talk about an investigation while it's under way," Frank said. He felt a little foolish saying that. In fact, he talked about his investigations all the time . . . but only with people he trusted.

Liz must have sensed what he really meant. Her cheeks turned pink, and she pressed her lips together tightly.

"If you want the latest," she said after a pause, "be sure to tune in this evening. Did you catch my segment last night?"

"Yes," Frank said. He kept his voice carefully neutral. Even so, her cheeks turned a deeper color.

"Yeah, I know," Liz blurted. "Nobody notices what happens on some dinky local show on public access cable. But this story could change that. Sooner or later people are going to start paying attention. And not just in Bayport either. A scandal like this could reach all the way to the state capital."

"Tell me, Liz," Frank said, "what makes you think the hockey team is involved in this business?"

"You know I can't talk about an investigation while it's under way," Liz said smugly. "I have a reliable source. That's all I'll say."

Callie came over and joined them. Liz gave her a cold look and walked away.

"Does she have a crush on you?" Callie asked. She sounded half peeved and half amused by the idea.

"I hope not," Frank replied. "My life is complicated enough already."

Frank looked past Callie. About twenty feet down the hall Carl Shute stood glaring at them. When he saw Frank notice him, he made a rude gesture. Frank ignored it. He also ignored the black sweatshirt with the grinning skull on it. He was much more interested in Carl's shoes. It was hard to be accurate at that distance, but Frank estimated they were about a size twelve.

With a sneer, Carl turned and stalked off down the hall.

The bell rang for class.

Joe's mother was waiting for him when he entered the house. "You should call the school," she said. "The principal's office has telephoned several times this morning."

Joe raised his eyebrows questioningly. "Any idea what they want?" he asked.

"I asked, of course," Mrs. Hardy said. "All they could tell me was that it was important for you to call as soon as possible."

Joe picked up the phone and dialed. Eventually he reached Mr. Chambers's secretary. When he told her his name, she said, "The principal has scheduled a meeting with you for noon today. Please be on time. He has a very crowded afternoon."

Joe really wished he could tell her that his afternoon was crowded too and that he didn't go to meetings that were scheduled without asking him. He repressed the impulse. Acting like a smart aleck would only damage his case.

Joe got to school at 11:52 and went directly to Mr. Chambers's office. Tony was already in the waiting area. He glanced up when Joe entered, then looked away. Obviously he was still ticked off at Joe and Frank.

Joe picked up a golf magazine and tried to get interested in it. It was mostly photos of guys in lime green slacks that clashed with the impossibly green grass on the course.

"You can go in now," the secretary said. She stood and pushed open the door to the inner office.

Mr. Chambers was seated behind his desk. A row of three chairs had been set out facing him. In another chair in the corner of the room sat Mr. Sheldrake, even more grim than usual.

Joe's heart sank. He hadn't really expected cake and balloons, but he had hoped the authorities might lighten up a bit once they'd had time to think over the facts.

Joe and Tony sat down. Chambers tented his fingertips, then tapped his chin with them. Looking at Joe and Tony over his half-moon reading glasses, he said, "This is a very unfortunate business."

Joe and Tony waited in silence.

"Very unfortunate," Chambers repeated. "However, it could have been worse. After a very thorough investigation, we have established that the copy of the test found in your possession was the only one missing from the shipment. Since that copy was still sealed, we are confident that the integrity of the test has not been compromised."

"Does that mean I can come back to school?" Tony asked eagerly. "I'm not on suspension anymore? Will this show up on my record?"

Chambers held up a hand like a cop directing traffic. "It's not quite that simple, I'm afraid."

Joe nodded. He'd had a hunch it wouldn't be that simple. It hardly ever was.

The principal picked up two sheets of paper and said, "All I need are your signatures on these agreements. Read them carefully first. Once you've signed, the suspensions will be lifted, and all mention of them will be wiped from your records."

Chambers handed them the documents. Joe skimmed his first, then reread it more slowly.

"Wait a minute," he said. His voice came out louder and shakier than he intended. "This thing's a confession! If we sign it, we're admitting we took the copy of the test as a prank. And we're agreeing not to talk about any of this publicly, including to the media."

"That's right," Chambers said.

"But that's *not* right," Tony protested. "It's like I told Mr. Sheldrake on Monday. I don't know how that test got in my backpack. I didn't take it, and I didn't put it there. Why should I say I did?"

"Look, Tony," Chambers said in a softer tone, "it's important to put these unfortunate events behind us. To draw a line and move on. That's all this document is meant to do. We know you didn't mean any real harm. Luckily no real harm was done. This is a recognition of that. It's a way to get past these difficulties and get on with what really counts, the business of education."

Joe cleared his throat. Taking a deep breath, he said, "No way will I sign this. It's all a lie. Tony didn't take that test, and neither did I. And I'll tell that to anybody I can get to listen!"

Chambers looked over at Sheldrake, then back at

Joe. "I'm sorry you take that attitude, Joe," he said. "I was warned that you might. I urge you to reconsider. What will it cost you to sign? After all, you and Tony *did* have the test. And do you really want to go around spreading dirt about an institution you should be proud to support?"

"I'm sorry too," Joe said, "but I won't sign." He tried to ignore the hollow feeling under his ribs.

"Very well," the principal said, leaning back in his chair and looking out the window. "You will remain on suspension, pending a disciplinary hearing. At that time a range of penalties may be considered, up to and including expulsion and the filing of criminal charges."

Chambers turned back to Tony. "Well, Tony," he said, "have you decided?"

"Um—" Tony said. His voice cracked. He stopped for a moment, then said, "Can I think it over? I want to talk to my mom and dad too. I can't decide something this important without them."

Joe noticed a damp mark on the document where Tony was gripping it.

"Of course, Tony," Chambers said. "Think it over. But I'm afraid we don't have all the time in the world. I must have your signature by Friday at noon. Joe, I'm going to offer you the same extension. I hope you will use the time to give serious consideration to your decision. Until then you both are still on suspension."

12 In the Slot

Joe and Tony left the building together. "You're not really thinking about signing that thing, are you?" Joe asked.

"Do I have a choice?" Tony asked bitterly. "If I sign, the whole business gets swept under the rug. If I don't, they come after me and ruin my life. Anyway, we're minors. It's not as if our signatures are legally binding."

Joe stopped and turned to look his friend in the eye. "Listen, Tony, straight out, did you have anything at all to do with taking that test?"

"Of course not!" Tony burst out. "I know you and Frank don't believe me."

"I do," Joe told him. "I know Frank does too. Then that settles it. You can't sign that paper. We've got to hang tough until we can uncover the truth."

"You think they care about the truth?" Tony demanded. "They want this settled, that's all. You heard Chambers. Draw a line, move on. Didn't anybody ever tell you how it works, Joe? If you want to get along, you have to go along!"

"Then I won't get along," Joe said stubbornly. "Somebody stole that test and planted it in your backpack. Probably half the school, teachers included, think you and I are cheaters. If we sign those papers, they'll *know* we are. Do you really think I'm going to stand for that? No way! We'll find out who took that test and why. And we'll make sure people know what we find out."

Before they separated, Tony promised to let Joe and Frank know before he did anything about signing the document.

Once again Joe's mother was waiting for him when he got home. Her face was grim.

"I just got off the phone with Mr. Chambers," she announced.

"Did he tell you about the confession he wanted me and Tony to sign?" Joe asked.

"He certainly did," Mrs. Hardy replied. "He asked me to talk some sense into you."

"What did you say?" Joe asked.

"I told him I couldn't speak for Tony's parents," Mrs. Hardy said firmly, "but as far as your father and I are concerned, if you say you weren't involved in this affair, you weren't. It would be wrong of you to sign a paper saying you were. I also said that if need be, we'd fight this in court. He was not pleased to hear that."

"Thanks, Mom," Joe said, giving her a hug. "I knew I could count on you. And don't worry. Frank and I are hot on the trail of the real culprit."

"That doesn't surprise me a bit," Mrs. Hardy said with a hint of a smile. "Oh, someone left an odd message for you on the answering machine."

Joe went over to the machine and pressed Play. The voice of Sal Martin boomed out into the room. "If you're the same Joe Hardy who was in my office yesterday, you know who this is. You can guess why I'm calling. My boys wanted to come after you for a little conversation, but I talked them out of it . . . *for now.*"

Joe made a face. Why hadn't anybody let him know today was going to be Threaten Joe Hardy Day?

"I've dropped the line of business we talked about," Martin said. "So there's no reason you and me should have any further dealings. I'm okay with that. You don't mess with me, I don't mess with you. But don't cross me, Joey, baby. If you do, I'll make sure you regret it."

"I can't say I liked the sound of that," Mrs. Hardy remarked.

"Me neither," Joe said. "I hate being called Joey. And 'Joey, baby,' is five times worse!"

Joe's stomach reminded him that he still had not had lunch. He went out to the kitchen and started to fix a sandwich. As he was spreading mustard on the bread, the phone rang. It was Frank.

"Hey, Biff says he saw you and Tony leaving school a little while ago," Frank said. "What's up?"

"We had a meeting with Mr. Chambers," Joe replied. He described what had happened.

"Those guys are the pits!" Frank exclaimed. "You know why they're trying so hard to get you to sign a confession? Because without it, they don't have any case at all. Hang in there, Joe!"

Joe then told Frank about the call from Sal Martin.

"That fits in with what Iola learned this morning," Frank said when he finished. "You see what this means?"

"Yeah, those thugs aren't going to break my knees for totaling their pickup," Joe said.

"That's good," Frank said. "That's very good. But what I meant was, if Martin pulled out, it's because he couldn't get a copy of the SAB. That means we can cross him off our list of suspects."

"So who does that leave?" Joe asked.

"Number one is some buddy of Brad Austin's," Frank replied. "It's pretty clear the test you guys found was meant to be put in Brad's backpack. If it had been, I don't suppose we'd have even known it was missing."

"I could have lived with that," Joe said dryly. "I'm

going to take a shower. After that meeting with Chambers and Sheldrake, I need it. I'll meet you in front of school at three-thirty. I have to turn in my homework first."

Frank hung up the phone. Callie was waiting next to him. As they walked to their next class, he filled her in on Joe's news.

"So we have less than two days to solve the case," Callie said when he finished. "Do you think we can pull it off?"

"I hope so," Frank replied. "We're getting somewhere."

"Do you mind if we stop by my locker?" Callie asked, brushing her hair back from her face. "I need a barrette."

"Sure thing," Frank replied. "It's on our way."

"I'll just be a sec," Callie told him as she entered her combination. She swung open the locker door and let out a piercing scream.

Frank rushed to her side. "What is it?" he asked anxiously. "What's wrong?"

"Look!" Callie exclaimed. She pointed inside the locker.

Callie's coat was hanging on a hook. The side facing the door had big gobs of red goo dripping down it.

Frank leaned closer. He recognized the tomatoey scent of ketchup. There was a folded paper on the floor of the locker. He picked it up and opened it.

"Watch out snooper!" it read. "Next time it'll be real blood!"

Frank showed Callie the note. "Whoever did this must have shoved it through the louver," he said. "And the same with the ketchup."

Callie's cry had attracted onlookers. One of them, a girl Frank didn't know, stepped forward and said, "I saw somebody hanging around here before my last class. He was acting kind of sneaky. That's why I noticed."

"What did he look like? Can you describe him?" Frank asked.

"I don't know," the girl said. "All I remember is, he had dark hair and big shoulders. Oh, yeah—he was wearing a black sweatshirt with a skeleton head on the front. Gross!"

Frank looked at Callie. They both recognized the description.

Carl Shute!

Joe was waiting in the van half a block from school. Frank yanked the door open and climbed into the passenger seat. "We're going to Sylvan Rink," he announced.

"Okay," Joe said, starting the engine. "Why?"

"The hockey team has practice there this afternoon," Frank replied. "I want a word with Carl

Shute." He told Joe about the ketchup attack on Callie's locker.

"Yuck! She must be upset," Joe said. "Do you want some backup?"

Frank shook his head. "I'll handle it," he said. "Anyway, you're still barred from talking to other students. You don't want to hand the administration anything they can hold over you."

At the skating rink Joe pulled in next to a beat-up red 4x4. Frank gave it a casual glance as he got out. Then his gaze sharpened. On the floor behind the driver's seat were two steel jerricans, the kind that had been used to ice the Hardys' driveway. A school notebook was on the backseat. Frank was not surprised to see the name Shute on it.

Inside the cavernous rink building the only activity was the Zamboni circling the ice, grinding down the grooves left by earlier skaters. Frank walked down to the low wooden barrier separating the rows of seats from the rink and looked around. Had practice been called off?

"Can I help you?" A man came out of the passageway that led under the stands. He wore a Bayport High School letter jacket with leather sleeves and a baseball cap.

Frank introduced himself and said, "I need to talk to Carl Shute."

"He and the other fellows are changing," the man

told him. "I'm Coach Frechette. Anything I can do?"

Frank gave him a puzzled look. "I thought the hockey coach was a different man."

"You're probably thinking of my assistant, Vernon Dobeny," Frechette said. "He has the afternoon off. Carl should be out in a minute."

"Okay, thanks," Frank said. He took a seat in the front row and watched the Zamboni. The man operating it steered a careful path that just overlapped the area he had already smoothed. Another three or four circuits, and the whole rink would be finished.

"What are you doing here?" someone demanded in an angry voice.

Brad Austin stared down at Frank. He was wearing his blue and red uniform. He had his skates slung over his shoulder and his stick in his hand.

Frank got to his feet. "I need to talk to Carl Shute," he repeated.

"You need to talk to *me*," Brad retorted. "Why are you guys picking on me? What did I ever do to you?"

"We're not picking on you," Frank said. "If anything, we're the ones getting picked on . . . by your buddies."

"Oh, yeah?" Brad said, sticking out his chin. "What do you call tipping off the security people that I had something illegal in my backpack? That's not picking on me? They must have spent twenty minutes searching me."

Frank's eyes widened. "When was this?" he asked eagerly.

"As if you didn't know," Brad replied. "On Monday, right after practice."

Frank stared. He was so engrossed by Brad's information that he barely noticed the other members of the hockey team filing into the arena.

"Brad," he said, "my brother and I had nothing to do with that. Listen, my brother got suspended because a stolen test turned up in his friend Tony's backpack at that exact time. Tony's pack looks just like yours. Don't you see? Somebody tried to frame *you*. But they ended up framing Tony and Joe by mistake!"

"That's crazy!" Brad said. "Who'd want to do that to me?"

"I don't know . . . yet," Frank told him. "But it's not me or Joe. No offense, but we never even heard your name before this week. Why would we—"

"Carl!" Brad shouted. "No, don't!"

Frank turned. Carl, holding his stick in both hands at chest height, cross-checked him. Frank recoiled. The wooden barrier caught him behind the knees, and he fell backward onto the ice.

Stunned, he turned his head and saw the Zamboni bearing down on him. The whirling blades that ground the ice smooth were only feet away from his face!

13 Freezing the Puck

"Look out!"

"Get him!"

"Quick!"

The shouts of alarm echoed through the empty arena.

Frank rolled onto his stomach and tried frantically to get to his feet. His hands and knees kept slipping on the ice.

Suddenly someone grabbed his right ankle and pulled. He felt himself slide backward over the ice, toward the safety of the barrier. His shirt rucked up, leaving his midsection bare. He felt as if his belly were being massaged with an ice cube.

The Zamboni operator had been concentrating on staying precisely in line with his earlier swath.

Alerted by the shouts, he threw his machine into neutral and glided to a stop. By then the Zamboni was so close to Frank that he could have reached out and touched it. He didn't.

A couple of people reached over the barrier. They grabbed Frank under the arms and lifted him into the stands. One, he saw, was Brad Austin.

"Thanks," Frank murmured. "I needed that."

"Okay, what's going on here?" Coach Frechette demanded angrily.

"This jerk has been pulling dirty tricks on Brad," Carl said, pointing at Frank. "I wanted to make him back off."

Frechette gave Frank a questioning look. "How about you?" he asked. "Anything to say?"

"I haven't done a thing to Brad," Frank said. "And you saw, Carl attacked me just now without any warning or provocation. But that's not all. Four of your players, armed with their hockey sticks, attacked me and my brother this morning near school. And last night somebody poured water on my family's driveway to create a sheet of ice. We almost had a serious accident."

Brad cleared his throat. "Uh, Coach?" he said. He sounded troubled. "It's true a lot of bad feelings have been stirred up against this guy and his brother. I don't know if there's any good reason for it. I do know it's there. Maybe some of the guys went a little too far, I don't know."

Frechette turned to Frank. "Can you identify the people you're accusing?" he asked. "Do you have any proof?"

"The guys who attacked us before school were wearing warm-up jackets and hockey masks," Frank replied. "No, I can't identify them."

"There, you see!" Carl exclaimed. "It's all garbage, what he's saying."

Frank glanced quickly at Carl's feet. He had not yet changed into his skates. His running shoes were at least a size twelve. Frank decided to take a risky chance.

"But," Frank said, in a carrying tone, "this morning I sketched the shoeprint of one of the people who iced our driveway. Here it is."

Frank opened his notebook to the page and handed it to Coach Frechette. "I'm willing to bet," he added, "that this matches Carl's shoe. And if you go out to the parking lot and check the jerricans in the back of his 4x4, I bet they still have a little water in them."

"Carl?" Frechette said.

"This is just another of his frames!" Carl declared uneasily.

"Would you mind showing me the bottom of your shoe?" the coach asked.

"Yes, I would mind," Carl shouted. "You'd take the word of this dork over the word of a member of your team? What kind of idiot are you?"

An instant later Frank saw Carl's face change as he realized he had gone too far.

"You're benched until further notice, Shute," Frechette said calmly. "Not for being insubordinate and insulting to me, but for assaulting a fellow student. You know I don't tolerate that conduct on or off the ice. You'd better leave now. And if I hear of any more trouble from you, you're off the team. Is that clear?"

"Yes, Coach," Carl said sullenly. He started for the exit. The glance he flashed at Frank promised vengeance.

Frechette turned to Frank. "You have my apology for what just happened," he said. "But on the whole, it might be best if you left too. This is an important practice, and your presence will not be helpful."

"I understand," Frank said.

He found his way outside to the van. On the drive home he gave Joe a detailed account of the events inside the skating rink. "So it's pretty clear," he said at the end. "Carl's been the ringleader. I don't understand *why* he started this campaign against us, but he did."

"I bet I know," Joe said. "On Sunday, when we were at the park, he was really obnoxious. He nearly banged into Callie. I went over and faced him down in front of his bud. He's probably been stewing over that ever since."

"You may be right. Bullies like him hate it when somebody calls their bluff. Anyway, we just learned something else really important. Brad Austin wasn't expecting to get that copy of the SAB. Believe me, I saw his face. He couldn't fool a two-year-old if he tried."

"You mean, it was meant to be a surprise?" Joe asked. "Like, 'Oh, look what some nice friend gave me for my birthday'?"

"That doesn't make sense," Frank said, frustrated. "Maybe it wasn't meant for Brad after all. Maybe it was supposed to go to someone else entirely, whose backpack looks just like Tony's and Brad's."

"And who left it on the floor of the gym during fourth period on Monday?" Joe asked skeptically. "And who kept his or her mouth shut when the test didn't show up as expected? It's possible, I guess, but— Frank!"

"What is it?" Frank asked, alarmed. He looked around. They were driving past school. Nothing seemed out of the ordinary.

"Up ahead," Joe said. "The car that just came out of the staff parking lot. That's the one I saw at the rendezvous with Sal Martin. I'm sure of it!"

Joe pressed the accelerator. He moved up until the van was only a couple of car lengths behind the old brown sedan. Frank wrote down the license number. Then he said, "If you pass him, I'll get a look at the driver."

"I will," Joe said.

Joe waited to let an oncoming car go by. Then he sped up and swung out to pass. As he started to pull alongside, the car's right-turn signal flashed, followed by the brake lights. A moment later the car made a fast right turn onto a side street.

Joe overshot the intersection. He pressed on the brakes, stopped, and backed up. Too late. The other car was already out of sight.

"Never mind," Frank said as Joe muttered insults to himself. "We've got his plate number. We can run it through the DMV database as soon as we get home."

When Frank and Joe reached their house, they were delighted to find Fenton Hardy in the living room with Mrs. Hardy.

"Hello, boys," he said heartily. "Am I ever glad to get home! I hear you've been having a little excitement here."

"I'll say we have," Frank replied. He and Joe took turns detailing their new case. When Joe got to his meeting with Mr. Chambers, his father's face darkened.

"Trying to force you to sign that statement is disgraceful," the famous detective said. "There's a saying in political circles: It's not the crime that does you in; it's trying to cover it up. Your principal could stand to learn that."

"I don't want to defend Mr. Chambers," Mrs. Hardy said, "but what if he really believes Joe and Tony are guilty? He may think he is offering them a way out."

"I don't think he cares if we're guilty," Joe burst out. "If he thought about it for one minute, he'd know we aren't. All he wants is to sweep this under the rug."

"But we're going to do our best to pull the rug out from under him," Frank said.

Mr. and Mrs. Hardy looked at each other. They both laughed.

"We're not laughing at you," Mr. Hardy said quickly. "We were just thinking that that rug is getting an awful lot of use!"

After a few minutes' more conversation, Frank and Joe excused themselves and went to the computer. Navigating through the state motor vehicles site was frustrating, but soon they had their answer. The brown sedan was registered to Ramon Mercado, at an address on Tulip Lane in Bayport.

"Ramon!" Frank exclaimed. "I bet that's the guy who works in Receiving! How many Ramons work at Bayport High School?"

"You mean the guy who tried to squash you and Callie under a load of school supplies?" Joe asked. "I think he has some explaining to do."

* * *

Tulip Lane was in an older neighborhood of big houses. Some of them needed repairs, but others had been recently renovated. Joe made one pass down Ramon's block without finding his address. On the way back, he realized the number was over the garage at the rear of another house. He parked on the street. He and Frank walked up the driveway, climbed a set of outside stairs, and knocked.

"Who is it?" The door opened a crack. Ramon peered out, recognized Frank, and tried to slam the door. Frank blocked it with his foot.

"What do you want with me?" Ramon demanded.

"Sal Martin," Joe said. "Tell us about Sal and the State Achievement test."

"I don't know what you're talking about!" Ramon blustered. "I don't know any Sal Martin."

"I saw you meet him yesterday," Joe said, stretching the facts a bit. "He asked you to get him a copy of the test, didn't he? You know you could lose your job and get in trouble with the law over this?"

Ramon turned pale. "Listen, guys," he said, opening the door wider, "let's say I heard a rumor somebody—no names—would pay big money for a copy of that test. Maybe I just wanted to check it out. No harm in that, is there?"

"That depends," Frank said.

Ramon spread his hands wide. "I didn't steal the test," he declared. "I couldn't if I'd wanted to. They would have been on to me right away. The cartons were sealed with this special tape."

"Let me get this straight," Joe said. "You're saying the cartons were still sealed when you locked them in the storeroom."

"That's right," Ramon said eagerly. "Then, on Monday morning, my boss found one of the cartons open. I couldn't have done it. I don't have the key."

"Who does?" Frank asked.

Ramon counted on his fingers. "My boss . . . and the principal's office . . . and the athletics department. They keep supplies in there. That's it, I think."

Joe and Frank went on questioning Ramon. In spite of their best efforts, they didn't learn anything more. At last they decided he had nothing more to tell them.

Back home Frank went to the telephone. He knew one of the assistant baseball coaches well enough to call him after school. When he got off the phone, he looked thoughtful.

"The key to the storeroom is kept in the drawer of one of the secretaries' desks," he reported to Joe. "Apparently all the coaches know where it is. They need to get to the supplies when they have practice after school and on weekends."

"Frank," Joe said, with a note of excitement, "remember the calls on Saturday that came from one of the school phones? I bet whoever made them stole the test from the storeroom at the same time."

"And I have a list of everybody who signed in," Frank said. "It may not tell us who's guilty, but it should help us figure out who isn't."

At seven the Hardys gathered around the television. Liz Webling got time on the cable program once again. Looking very serious, she said, "In our ongoing hard news investigation of the Bayport High School cheating scandal, we have learned from a highly placed staff member that some of the school's hockey team may be deeply involved. Informed sources tell us that one or more essential players may have had academic problems lately. It is thought that the crucial State Achievement test was stolen for their benefit. School officials refused to comment."

"This girl will go far," Fenton Hardy commented with a smile. "How many viewers will notice that she didn't give us a single solid fact?"

"She gave us one," Frank said, "if it's true. She's getting leads from a highly placed staff member. I'd give a lot to know—"

With a heart-stopping crash, one of the front windows shattered, spraying the room with splinters of glass.

14 Slap Shot!

After a moment of stunned silence, Aunt Gertrude let out a scream. Joe jumped to his feet and ran across the room. He reached the front window one stride ahead of Frank. The curtains billowed as cold air poured in through the broken pane. Joe pushed them aside and stared out into the night.

From the street came the clamor of a car's engine at full throttle. As it faded, he caught a glimpse of a 4x4 speeding past the streetlight up the block.

"Carl Shute," Frank muttered through clenched teeth. "I should have known he'd try to get back at us!"

Mrs. Hardy took Aunt Gertrude's hand and patted it. "It's all right," she murmured. "No one's hurt, thank goodness. A broken window can be fixed."

Mr. Hardy bent down, then said, "Our unexpected caller left this behind." A hockey puck nestled in his outstretched hand. "Something to do with your case, I assume?"

"I'm afraid so," Frank said, taking the puck.

"We'll clean up the mess," Joe added.

Joe and Frank swept and vacuumed the broken glass off the living room floor. Joe found a piece of foam-core posterboard in the workroom. They cut it to size and taped it in place of the missing pane. Then they went out to the kitchen for milk and freshly baked butterscotch raisin cookies.

"There's something very peculiar about this case," Frank said. "Usually, when people are up to something, they try to hide who they are. Here they're practically beating us over the head with it."

"How do you mean?" Joe asked, brushing cookie crumbs from the front of his shirt.

"Those guys who attacked us," Frank replied, "they could have worn ski masks and carried baseball bats. But no, they wore hockey masks and team jackets and carried hockey sticks. Just now, did Carl throw a rock through our window, like any reasonable person? Unh-unh—a hockey puck. When dear Liz gets a tip from someone, what's it about? Hockey! Whoever's in back of this has done everything except put up a neon sign that blinks 'Hockey! Hockey! Hockey!'"

"You know what else?" Joe said. "Chambers and

Sheldrake are doing their best to sweep the whole business under the rug. The main reason it hasn't worked is that somebody keeps pulling it *out* from under the rug! You know those phone calls to sell copies of the SAB? I think they were phonies. Their real purpose was to spread the word that copies of the test were for sale. But they weren't, not really. That kid you talked to who tried to buy one couldn't. And I told you what Chambers said. Only one copy of the SAB was missing . . . the one that turned up in Tony's backpack."

Frank jumped up and paced the room. "You see what that means, Joe? The whole point of stealing the test must have been to have it found. But not in Tony's pack. In Brad Austin's! That's why the guards were tipped off that he was carrying something illicit. So he'd be caught with the test!"

"It all fits," Joe said excitedly. "But why? And who? Does somebody hate Brad enough to pull such a complicated stunt? Why not simply catch him in a dark alley and beat him up?"

"Two facts," Frank said. "Brad is a key player—maybe *the* key player—on the Bayport hockey team, and Bayport has its most important game of the season coming up next week, against New Harbor. Fit those facts together and—"

"Brad is framed, he gets suspended and can't play, and Bayport loses the conference title!" Joe shouted, leaping up from his seat. He and Frank exchanged high fives. "Now all we need to do is find someone who's working secretly for New Harbor."

"Someone who has access to the storeroom, who was in the school building on Saturday, and who has influence over the members of the hockey squad," Frank said.

Joe looked at him with growing understanding.

"I think we have a good idea who that somebody is." Frank continued. "What we need now is evidence that might convince someone in authority. Here's the way I think we should play it tomorrow. . . ."

Frank and Joe left the house early the next morning and drove to Tony's. He had called late the night before and asked them to come by before school. He needed to talk to them.

Tony met them at the front door and took them back to the breakfast nook again. There was a plate of doughnuts on the table. Tony poured three glasses of milk and sat down.

"Okay, guys," he said. "Tell me what I have to do."

"Stay in there," Frank said. A little milk had spilled on the table. He used his index finger to draw patterns in it. "Try to take it easy."

"Easy for you to say," Tony retorted. "Nobody's trying to hang *you* by your thumbs. My mom and dad think I should sign and put the whole thing behind me. Maybe they're right. How much hassle do I need? If I go in there tomorrow and tell Chambers I'm not signing, he'll throw the book at me."

"Maybe not," Joe said. "Look, the last thing they want is bad publicity. So far the only one talking about this in public is Liz Webling, on that cable show. She keeps trying to make it into a big story, but so far it hasn't worked."

"Even her dad's newspaper hasn't printed a word about it," Frank added. "I think that's because at this point it's only rumors. But if Chambers takes any more action against you guys, I promise you he's facing a very messy court case. That will hit the papers for sure. No, I think they're bluffing."

"Boy, do I wish I could believe that!" Tony said. "But I don't know if I want to try them. I can just hear what my mom and dad will say if I tell them they need to hire me a lawyer."

Inspired by Frank's example, Joe was doodling on a piece of paper he had found on the table. Now he looked more closely at it. It was a store receipt for six pairs of cushion foot socks.

"Oh, sorry," he said, sliding it over to Tony. "You sure go through a lot of socks, don't you?"

Tony glanced at it. "That's not mine," he said casually. "It was in my backpack. I don't know how it got there. I haven't bought socks in months."

Joe stared at him. In his mind, he saw Tony pulling a plastic-wrapped booklet from his backpack and brushing a slip of paper off its front.

"This was stuck to the SAB!" Joe exclaimed. "It must have been in your pack since Monday. With luck, it'll lead us straight to the person who stole the test!"

The three friends studied the slip. It was from a well-known sporting goods store and dated the previous Saturday morning.

"Do you think a clerk would remember such a measly sale?" Joe asked.

"It depends," Frank said. "If our fellow's a regular customer . . ."

Joe borrowed an envelope from Tony and tucked the slip inside. "Why don't you come along?" he asked. "This may be the last lap of the case. You deserve to be in on it."

Tony shook his head. "Sorry, guys," he said. "I wish I could, but I'm still grounded."

As they drove off, Joe saw Tony at the window, watching.

At school Joe maneuvered the van into a spot near the entrance to the staff parking lot. He and Frank settled down to watch the cars streaming in.

"What if we miss him?" Joe asked. "Maybe he'll be late. Maybe he's already here."

"Then we'll figure out some other way to tag him," Frank said. "Let's worry about that when we need to."

It was only a few minutes before first period when Frank sat up straighter and said, "There. That's him."

"Where?" Joe asked.

"The blue SUV waiting to make a left," Frank replied. "Look at that. He's wearing a parka the same color as his car."

"That clinches it!" Joe exclaimed. "I didn't tell you, did I? That's exactly the way the woman in the gas station described the guy who made the phone calls trying to sell the test."

Frank hurried into class. Joe waved to a couple of kids he knew and drove home to enjoy a relaxed second breakfast. At moments like this he wasn't 100 percent sure he *wanted* his suspension lifted.

The sporting goods store was just opening when Joe arrived. He went inside and asked to speak to the manager. A woman with short black hair came over. "I'm Ms. Kazakas," she said. "How can I help you?"

"My buddy found a package of socks in the parking lot of the mall," Joe said. "They must have fallen out of a car. He was going to keep them, but then he saw this slip in the bag and thought maybe he could track the owner."

The manager eyed him sharply. Joe knew she thought *he* was the finder. Then she took the register slip. "Saturday morning," she murmured. "Arnie made the sale. He might remember. . . . Arnie? A word?"

A blond guy who looked as if he spent a lot of time in the weight room came over. Ms. Kazakas explained. Arnie studied the slip and wrinkled his forehead. "Socks . . . Saturday . . . Oh, sure. I had a long conversation with the guy about the Stanley Cup. He really knows his hockey."

"Do you know his name?" Joe asked eagerly. "Can you describe him?"

"His name? No," Arnie replied. "As for what he looks like, he's in pretty good shape. Barrel chest, powerful arms. I didn't notice much more than that. Oh, and he has really bushy eyebrows."

At two minutes to noon, Frank rushed out of school and jogged over to where Joe was parked.

"We're on," Frank said breathlessly. "I called the athletics office half an hour ago. He's got a lunch meeting off campus."

"We don't *know* it hooks up with the case," Joe said.

"No," Frank agreed. "But if we're right about his scheme, today is critical. He's bound to do something, at lunch or afterward. Oops, here he comes. Duck!"

Joe slid down in his seat until the blue SUV drove out of the lot and turned east. Then he sat up and started after their quarry. A few minutes later they were speeding along the interstate. The miles clicked by.

"Where's he going?" Joe complained. "Boston?"

The SUV's right-turn signal started to flash. It took the next off-ramp. A mile farther along, it turned into the lot of a diner and stopped near the door. Joe pulled the van into a slot directly across from the front of the diner. He and Frank climbed into the back and settled down next to the rear windows.

"There he is," Frank said after a few moments. "Third window from the left. He's with a man with gray hair and a mustache."

Before leaving home, Joe had packed a gear bag with binoculars and a telephoto-equipped 35-mm camera. He handed the binoculars to Frank while he focused the camera. The reflections off the diner's window made for tricky picture-taking, but after ten minutes he was confident he had some good, clear shots of the two men inside.

The lunch meeting seemed to drag on and on. Finally the two men left. Outside the diner they stopped to shake hands. Joe clicked off frame after frame.

"I hope I'm not burning film on shots of him with his chiropractor," Joe murmured.

"Uh-oh," Frank said.

Turning away from his companion, their quarry had noticed the Hardys' van. For a long moment he stared in their direction. Joe used the chance to take a great head shot. Then their target returned to the SUV.

Joe and Frank switched their attention to the gray-haired man. He walked over to a black German luxury sedan and got in. As he backed out, Joe snapped several pictures of the car that included the license plate.

"Okay, now what?" Joe asked urgently, dropping the camera into the gear bag. "Which one do we follow?"

"Neither," Frank said. "We go back to Bayport and get that film developed and printed. And we find out who the guy with the mustache is. We already know the most important thing about him."

"What?" Joe asked. "That he drives an expensive car?"

"Not that," Frank replied. "I'm talking about the decal in his back window. The one with the crossed hockey sticks and the words New Harbor Hornets!"

15 To the Penalty Box

Mr. Chambers looked silently at each of the three students in the chairs facing his desk. When his gaze reached Frank, his frown deepened.

"I invited you to this conference, Frank," he said, "because your brother felt so strongly about it. But I'm afraid I don't understand what your role is supposed to be."

"I'm here to help Joe," Frank said.

Chambers picked up a pencil and tapped the eraser end rhythmically on the desktop. "Hmm, yes," he said. "Well, our goal here this morning is to assign and accept responsibility for the breach of security that occurred this week with respect to the State Achievement Battery. *Apparent* breach, I should say. Fortunately no actual breach took place. Tony, Joe, would you please give me the signed statements we discussed on Wednesday?"

Tony's eyes shifted in Joe's direction. Joe took a deep breath and said, "No, sir. Those statements are not correct. We'd like to explain to you what really happened."

Chambers, cool to begin with, became icy. "I don't have time to waste on charades," he declared.

"Then let's look at some facts," Frank said. "The sealed cartons containing the SAB tests were delivered to school last Thursday. We can show they were still sealed with a special security tape when they were put in a locked storeroom. By the way, neither Joe nor Tony has access to a key to that storeroom. Your office does, and Receiving, and the athletics department. By Monday one of the cartons had been opened and a test had been taken."

"To turn up later in the possession of Tony and Joe," Chambers said, breaking in. "Which is the point of that statement I expect them to sign."

"Tony's backpack was near another one just like it," Joe said. "And somebody had tipped off the guards to search the other guy's backpack at the exact same time Tony found the test in *his* backpack. Don't you see? Somebody tried to frame this other student, but it didn't work because the framer put the stolen test in the wrong backpack!"

For the first time Frank saw a trace of doubt in

the principal's expression. "Who is this other student?" he asked.

"Brad Austin," Joe said.

"That's ridiculous," Chambers said. "I know Brad. He is an upstanding young man and a fine athlete. I've recommended him for an athletic scholarship at the university I graduated from."

"What would have happened if a copy of the SAB had been found in his pack on Monday?" Frank asked.

"We would have had no choice," Chambers replied. "He would have been suspended while we tried to find out the facts."

"And Bayport's hockey team would have lost to New Harbor next week," Tony said.

"Are you suggesting—" Chambers asked.

"In the last few days," Frank told him, "there's been one incident after another connected to the hockey team. The only explanation that fits is that somebody—*somebody here at Bayport*—is trying to make sure New Harbor wins."

"I can't believe that!" Chambers declared.

Joe pulled out a close-up of the gray-haired man he had photographed the day before. "Do you know this man, Mr. Chambers?"

"Why, yes," replied the principal, who looked bewildered. "I've met him several times. He's Julius Perrone, the CEO of an electronics firm based in New Harbor. He's also a rabid hockey fan. What of it?"

"I took this picture yesterday," Joe said. "He was meeting in an out-of-the-way place with a member of the coaching staff of Bayport's hockey team."

"I can't believe that!" Chambers exclaimed. "Even if you're correct, there may be a perfectly innocent explanation."

"Sir, would you mind asking Mr. Frechette and Mr. Dobeny to come in?" Frank requested. "Also, there's a student named Liz Webling in your waiting room who has some valuable information to offer."

"You planned this whole thing," Chambers said accusingly. "It's a setup!"

"Sure, we planned it," Tony said. "We had to. We were in a tight place. But that doesn't mean we're trying to put one over on you. It's the straight stuff we're dishing out."

Chambers pinched his lower lip between his index finger and thumb while he thought. Then he reached for the phone. He told his secretary to get the two hockey coaches over right away and to send Liz in.

Liz came in and took the seat next to Tony. She gave Frank a smug look. No wonder, he thought. Not only did she have an exclusive on a big story, but she was also getting a chance to act like a real investigative reporter, not just a repeater of rumors.

There was a long, awkward silence while the group waited for Frechette and Dobeny to show up. Finally the office door swung open. The two coaches came in and looked with puzzlement at the lineup of students.

"I'm sorry to break in on your schedule like this," Chambers said. He motioned the coaches to two vacant chairs. "Some serious allegations have been made that concern the hockey program."

"Did these allegations come from the Hardy brothers?" Dobeny asked. "If so, you should know that they've recently gotten involved in a feud with some of our players. I've tried to keep it down, in line with our school policy on violence. But if you taunt one of my guys enough, he'll react."

Chambers looked at Frechette. "Coach?"

Frechette rubbed his chin. "I had to bench one of my starting players just yesterday for being involved in a fight with Frank Hardy. I don't know about the other incidents."

Frank's heart sank. Would Chambers believe the picture that was being painted? Of course he would. He already saw the Hardys as troublemakers. Their reputation as detectives wouldn't help. There was nothing a school official disliked more than trouble-makers.

"Coach Frechette," Frank said, "who started that fight?"

"It looked as though Carl made an unprovoked attack on you," Frechette replied. "Of course I don't know what may have led up to it."

"We don't have time to quibble about side issues," Chambers declared. "Let's get to the point. You boys accused one of my staff members of disloyal behavior. That's a very serious charge. You'd better be able to support it."

"Yes, sir," Joe said. "Well, once we figured out that the stolen test had been meant for Brad, we tried to find out who'd put it there. Somebody was calling Bayport students, offering to sell them copies of the test—"

"Outrageous!" Chambers exclaimed, slapping his palm on his desk.

"Yes, sir," Joe said again. "I tracked down the calls and got a description of the caller. It fits one of the hockey coaches. At that point we thought the object was to help Brad pass the SAB. But then why slip it in his pack, which was really Tony's pack? Why not just hand it to him?"

"Then, on Wednesday morning, a bunch of hockey players jumped us," Frank said. "We think somebody put them up to it."

"I stopped that fight, if you remember," Dobeny said.

"That's right, you did," Frank said. "A wonderful coincidence that you came along at just the right time. That was one of the things that made Joe and me take a much closer look at you, Coach Dobeny. When you went to your lunch date yesterday, we followed you."

Dobeny's face grew taut. He looked straight ahead and said nothing.

"What's this about lunch dates?" Chambers demanded. "I'm not going to put up with a lot of diversions from you, Frank."

"Here," Joe said. He produced an enlargement of his photo of Dobeny and Perrone in the diner parking lot, shaking hands. Chambers looked at it and turned pale. He passed it to Coach Frechette.

"Vernon, what's this?" Frechette asked. "Why did you meet with this man? You know he is the biggest fan of our biggest rival."

Dobeny straightened his shoulders. "I didn't tell you because I wanted it to be a surprise," he said. He took a deep breath. "Sure, Mr. Perrone is crazy about hockey. That's how I met him, at a hockey league dinner. I went to him with an idea, to set up a foundation to promote hockey in our area. He liked my plan, but I know he hates any kind of negative publicity. I just hope these boys' interference hasn't spoiled the deal."

Frank looked over at Liz and nodded.

"At Frank's suggestion, I interviewed Julius Perrone this morning by telephone," Liz announced. "I told him the upcoming game between Bayport and New Harbor was stirring a lot of interest in high school ice hockey. I asked for his comments."

Liz reached into her bag and took out a digital audio recorder. She found the spot she wanted on the tape and turned up the volume. A strong, assertive man's voice filled the room.

"The Hornets will romp all over Bayport next week," he said. "But that's just the beginning. I'm busy creating an organization to encourage hockey among grade school kids. By the time they reach high school age, they'll already be trained, experienced players."

"That sounds like an ambitious program," Liz's voice said.

"You bet it is," Perrone replied. "I don't believe in doing things halfway. I'm going to make New Harbor a hockey powerhouse, not just in our area but nationwide. I met only yesterday with the man I've picked to head up this effort. I can't tell you his name yet, but when we make the announcement next month, I guarantee it'll rock the hockey establishment in our region!"

Liz turned off the recorder and looked at Dobeny. "That doesn't quite fit in with what you said, Coach," she observed. "Any comments?"

"It's a difference in interpretation," Dobeny said, his voice rising. "If my plans go through, it'll be a boost to hockey throughout the area, including Bayport, of course. If Mr. Perrone wants to see this effort mainly in terms of New Harbor, that's his privilege."

Frank went on the attack. "There's no way to know what you might do in the future, Coach," he said, "but we do know what you've done already. You tried to get your best player suspended, by stealing a test and planting it in what you thought was his backpack."

"Prove it!" Dobeny shouted.

Joe held up a slip of paper. "When you put the test in Tony's bag by mistake, you didn't notice this stuck to the plastic. It's a register receipt from Saturday, for athletic socks. The clerk who made the sale can identify you."

Dobeny looked wildly around the room, then stared at the floor.

Frechette looked over at the principal, then said, "Vernon, I'd like you to take a leave of absence while we sort out this business. I really hope there's some innocent explanation for all this. But I warn you. If there isn't, if you really did what you've been accused of, I'll do my best to see that you never work in hockey again!"

It was the closing minute of play, and the game was tied 1–1. All the fans in the arena were on their feet. New Harbor drove toward the Bayport goal. At what seemed like the last moment, a Bayport guard with bright red hair moved in.

"Interception!" the announcer shouted. "Interception by number thirty-two, Waxman. He takes it down the ice. He slips through the Hornets' defense. Austin is in the clear. . . . He takes the pass. . . . He shoots. . . . Goal! Brad Austin makes his second goal of the game! And there's the buzzer! Bayport wins!"

In the stands Frank and Joe exchanged high fives, then gave Callie and Iola big hugs. All four were wearing the jerseys that had been given to them when they were made honorary members of the Bayport High School hockey team.

Liz Webling appeared, holding a digital camcorder. She aimed it at Frank and Joe. "As our viewers know," she said in a stage voice, "tonight's star, Brad Austin, was the target of a plot that was exposed right here on Channel Sixty-one. I'm with Frank and Joe Hardy, who helped uncover the conspiracy against the Bayport High School hockey team."

Frank looked at Joe and rolled his eyes. So now they were Liz's assistants!

"Joe," Liz said, "how does it feel to know that you had some small part in making tonight's victory possible?"

"This win is totally awesome," Joe said, grinning at the camera. "But let's be real. You and I aren't the ones who beat New Harbor tonight. It's Brad and the rest of the team who deserve the credit."

Looking a bit cross, Liz swung the camcorder to focus on Frank. "Anything you want to add, Frank?" she asked.

"It's a great night for Bayport High," Frank said enthusiastically. "As for those who tried to sway the results by crooked means, the outcome is pretty obvious. We iced them!"

BRUCE COVILLE'S

The fascinating and hilarious adventures of
the world's first purple sixth grader!

 A MINSTREL® BOOK

Published by Pocket Books   2304-06